RUBICON

A HWA SHORT STORY COLLECTION

Published in 2019 by Sharpe Books.

CONTENTS

Welcome to Rubicon

War, poetry, romance, mystery, exiles, kings and pirates - you'll find them all in this remarkable anthology of complete short stories, all of which are set in Ancient Rome and its far-flung Empire.

The Historical Writers' Association has put together this collection to showcase just some of the fantastic storytelling available today which focuses on Rome and to introduce readers to a whole library of gripping works by our authors. We are here to champion historical writing in all its rich variety, and to champion each other. This collection is part of that mission. The astonishing range of characters and voices you'll find in these pages will take you on a journey stretching from Hadrian's Wall to the temples of Egypt, from the very centre of power to backwaters surviving on the fringes of the known world, full of blood, passion, dark humour and moments of grace.

Whatever you like to read, we hope you'll find a new favourite author on these pages, and also get to learn something about these fantastic writers. You'll find interviews here with each of them so as well as enjoying their work, you can discover something about who they are and how they write, and why Rome as a subject continues to resonate and fascinate into the 21st century. Palace intrigues, the brutality of battle, revenge, faith, kindness and the strange workings of fate are all bursting out of this slim volume, we do hope you enjoy it.

You can read articles by and about our authors of fiction and non-fiction as well as getting writing advice and reading reviews on www.historiamag.com and you can see the breadth of our community on www.historicalwriters.org. We'd love to see you there.

Imogen Robertson
Chair, Historical Writers' Association.

Maker of Gold - Nick Brown

Panopolis, Egypt, 298 AD

In many ways, the day started well: I awoke from a restful, uninterrupted sleep; enjoyed a hearty breakfast of bread, cheese and dates with my wife; and was ready to depart by the second hour. But as I opened the front door, my mother-in-law darted out of the kitchen and gripped my arm. I knew what was coming.

'A dream, Zosimos.'

I tried not to show my displeasure. On the whole, I have no objection to my wife's mother; nor the practice of interpreting dreams. However, when one hears of such things on a weekly basis, one becomes rather less convinced of their significance. Her dreams often took the form of premonitions and I must admit that she had accurately predicted several events in the past. In recent times, however, few of her imaginings had materialised.

'Mother, I must go.'

'It was clear, so very clear. A man, clad in red.' She gazed up at me, green eyes unblinking.

'Is that all?'

'He will come to you.'

'And?'

'Whether he means ill or good, I cannot say.'

My house is situated only a short walk from the Temple of Min. I was glad I'd chosen my lighter tunic, for the day was a warm one; the sun clear and bright, the sky free of cloud. I had much planned for the next few days, and with the natural signs so favourable, my chances of success were good.

I can say without an excess of pride that I am a well-known person in my city, and as usual I exchanged greetings with many. The second half of my route took me along the Avenue of Septimius Severus. I heard the familiar cracks and thuds of

1

the stone-cutters within their great yard and it was here that I saw a Christian man whose name I could not recall. We exchanged a nod, for our paths had crossed once or twice at social functions. He looked nervous; no surprise given the Emperor's attitude towards his people, which was increasingly echoed by my fellow Egyptians. I did not share such hostility, perhaps because I'd spent much of my life studying the works of fellow practitioners from various faiths.

As I turned off the avenue towards the temple, a caravan passed by: dozens of heavily-laden camels guided by weary riders. Judging by the amount of sand stuck to them, they were not long from the desert.

As always, I stopped at the one place on my route where I could see the bountiful Nile. Even this brief sight of the brilliant waters brought a smile to my face.

The Temple of Min is one of the greatest holy places in the whole of Egypt, and the largest building in my city. Min is a god of fertility, worshipped here for centuries. In the time before the Greeks, the city was Khent-Min, but to them the god was Pan, hence the change of name. The temple is painted blue, and almost every surface is decorated with images of gods and birds and animals. I passed through the chill shadows of the broad, high entrance, where craftsmen were etching a poem in the stone.

I did not intend to tarry long, for the priests tend to make considerable demands on my time. Many outsiders consider *me* a priest – for there are divine aspects to my work – but I consider myself an artisan, and my official title is *master craftsman*. I simply could not begin the day without praying to Min so I hurried to the central shrine and knelt before the granite statue. Realising that I had not brought a votive for some weeks, I resolved to do so on the following day.

Once out of the shrine, I proceeded towards the rear of the temple and the vast walled compound where myself and hundreds of others are employed. Within the temple itself are chambers for priests, administrators, librarians, healers, embalmers, musicians and astronomers. In the compound are the craftsmen: bakers, beekeepers, weavers, builders and metalsmiths such as myself.

Upon seeing High Priest Hermaios hurrying towards me, I struggled not to grimace, as I'd hoped to at least begin my day's work without interruption. Such is the life of a master craftsman.

'Master Zosimos, may the gods favour you this day.'

'May they favour you, High Priest Hermaios.'

With his tall frame, hairless head and spotless white robes, Hermaios cut a striking figure. I sometimes felt rather inferior in my drab grey tunic but I cannot say that the high priest and his compatriots treated me in such a way, for they grasped the practical realities of my work.

Hermaios spoke softly, as pious men often do. 'I mentioned you and your labours this morning in my prayers. I gave an offering to great and honoured Thoth, so that he too might aid your efforts.'

'My thanks.'

'There are three issues I must mention.'

Hermaios often employed this opening; I suppose it helped him remember.

'Of course,' said I, affecting a patient manner.

Around us, the compound was already busy, and I noted the weavers overseeing a delivery of freshly-cut rushes.

'The order for Gargonius,' said Hermaois. 'It will be ready for the end of the month?'

'Indeed, it will.' I had already given my superiors numerous assurances on this matter. Gargonius was a Roman merchant with a fleet of ships that ran between Panopolis and Alexandria. He had asked for a dozen small statues of the Roman gods to decorate his new villa. Though I cared more about my research than profit, it was important that my guild fulfilled such contracts. These earnings formed a significant part of the temple's revenue and funded my work.

'Good,' said Hermaios. 'And have you spoken to Mersis today?'

'No.'

3

'Please do. The astronomers report an unexpected change in the ninth constellation.'

This was not a significant concern for me. Over the years, I had concluded that the position of the sun and the moon were of more significance to the sacred art than the stars.

'Thank you for notifying me. The third matter?'

Hermaois sighed. 'Yesterday we were visited by Timon, representative of the Temple of Dendara. They are supporting Nelios and his new guild.'

Nelios was a fellow practitioner of the sacred art who I had known for several years. He'd originally joined me as an apprentice at the Temple of Min but, over time, acrimony had developed between us. Though initially eager to learn, the young man proved difficult to educate. While my efforts were based largely on the texts of those that came before me, Nelios was dismissive of such research and relied too much on haphazard experimentation.

He had left the temple two years ago to form his own guild. While not yet in a position to threaten mine, his boastful character and bold claims ensured that his was a name I often heard.

'Well,' said I, 'that is their problem.'

'I suppose so.' Hermaois paused, evidently choosing his next words carefully. 'But Timon expressed … disappointment at your criticism of Nelios. In these matters, your opinion is greatly respected.'

'Believe me, I would prefer not to ever mention the man. But his manner and methods are detrimental to the art. I do not ask other practitioners to follow me; I merely advise them not to follow *him*.'

Hermaois held up his hands to appease me. 'And there can be no doubting your knowledge in such matters. But relations between ourselves and the Temple of Dendera are currently good, which gives everyone in Panopolis a better chance of ensuring the continuance of our ways. The current governor seems to respect our traditions but there's no telling what may change in Rome.'

'Understood. If I am asked my opinion of Nelios, I will give it. Otherwise, I shall not mention him at all.'

'Very well.' The high priest placed his hand on my arm. 'Master Zosimos, please know that we are all fully aware how lucky we are to have you. I shall not keep you a moment longer.'

One of my five assistants was ill with a fever, and three had been temporarily seconded to the temple to assist with some painting. That left me with Kastor, the youngest but most enthusiastic of the five, and I felt confident we would still be able to achieve much.

My main workshop is large: thirty paces by twenty, with a dozen circular windows to provide plenty of light. The building is constructed of mud-brick, which resists fire well and provides a consistent temperature. I was pleased to find that Kastor had already started the furnace and added another layer to Gargonius' statues. I took one outside and held it up to the light. The apprentice had perhaps used a little too much oil in the mixture but I said nothing. Kastor had only been with me for a few months, and though he'd rather been foisted upon me (as the son of an eminent priest), I couldn't fault his efforts so far.

Before carrying out the main task of the day, the young man and I knelt upon a sunlit patch of floor. I instructed Kastor to conduct the invocation, in which we appealed to the gods, the daimons and the elements. Through this we sought to harmonize our bodies and minds with the natural and the divine.

Once the invocation was complete, I inspected a delivery of bronze, which had recently arrived from a new supplier. I intended to heat a sample and remove the surface layer of copper. Only then could I begin to understand the characteristics of this particular alloy.

While we waited for the furnace to reach the appropriate temperature, Kastor cleared his throat. 'Master Zosimos, might I ask a question?'

'Do I not always say that you should?'

'You do, sir.' The young man scratched his cheek, then nodded at the sheets of metal. 'We are producing what some call Corinthian bronze – that is bronze transformed into gold.'

'On this occasion, yes.'

'And you are educating us in the other methods of altering substances to create gold.'

'Indeed.'

'Yet we also work with *pure* gold – the metal mined from the earth.'

'And how can we tell what is gold?'

Kastor counted the five markers on his fingers. 'Extreme weight, yellow colour, shine, resistance to marking, resistance to fire.'

'Precisely. What you refer to as "pure gold" demonstrates these characteristics more robustly than Corinthian bronze, smelted orpiment or any of the other materials. But there is no reason not to consider them variations of gold. All are the gifts of the gods.'

From the temple came the familiar sound of drums and bells. I glanced down at my hands, now illuminated and warmed by a shaft of sunlight.

'We who study the sacred art are part of a great, ongoing endeavour. We could not work without those who came before us; and those who come after us will build on our achievements. That is why we must be rigorous with our observations and record-keeping. I believe there will come a time where men like us will develop the ability to create what is currently only given to us by the gods of the earth.'

I was pleased by the expression on the young man's face; and the fact that he'd noticed the furnace was in need of more fuel.

'Sir, shall I-'

'Please.'

I turned my attention to the bronze. When the furnace flared, I spied some spotting in the metal that looked like arsenic. Once Kastor had finished adding firewood, I called him over.

'There is a volume by Bolus of Mendes that includes a section on impurities I'd like to consult. I believe it's the eighth. Can you fetch a copy from the library?'

'Of course, Master.'

'Kastor, don't ask Librarian Eugenios – his eyesight is terrible.'

I was about to begin heating the sample of bronze when I heard footsteps behind me.

'That was quick,' said I, assuming it was Kastor. But upon turning around, I found myself face to face with a stranger.

The man was difficult to age. He looked to me like a desert tribesman, for he was clad in black robes, his face lined and worn. Despite his weathered features, there was not a trace of grey within his thick beard.

'You are Zosimos.'

He spoke in halting Latin, his mouth ugly with jagged, yellow teeth. I was relieved to see no trace of a weapon.

'Who are you?' said I.

'Do not matter.'

'You waited for Kastor to leave – until I was alone.'

'Yes. This temple busy.' As the tribesman walked forward, he put both hands up, as if ready to attack. My eyes were drawn to one of his long, baggy sleeves, for I thought I'd seen something move under the cloth.

'Why are you here?'

'Send message. You talk about others. Too much.'

I recalled my mother-in-law's warning. Here was a man clad in black instead of red, but his intentions were clearly not good. I could hardly believe that even Nelios was capable of such an outrage but surely he – or some ally – was behind this.

I backed across the workshop, between two tables. The stranger followed me. I have seen eyes like his before: soldiers, warriors, those for whom violence is nothing more than work.

'Need to keep quiet.'

Now I clearly saw his left sleeve bulge. There was something alive in there.

'You see her? My girl.'

The man reached into the sleeve with his right hand and brought out a small snake: eyes a hateful black, slender purple tongue scouring the air. It was close enough for me to see the individual scales of a burnished pale red.

'Spitting cobra,' said the tribesman. 'Won't kill. But will blind. Hard to work then, no?'

I continued my retreat, and now looked around for something to defend myself.

The stranger stretched out his arm. The snake's head bobbed from side to side, its cold gaze fixed on me.

'If I were you, I'd put that thing away.'

This calm yet authoritative voice spoke in immaculate Greek, with the accent of a distinguished Roman. Dragging my gaze from the cobra, I saw a tall man stride into my workshop. Behind him were two legionaries.

The tall man drew his sword, closely followed by the soldiers. The three polished blades gleamed orange from the light of the furnace.

'Quickly now,' said the Roman, 'or I'll have my men chop that thing's head off.'

The tribesman looked back at him.

'If I have to ask again, it won't be the snake's head.'

The tribesman returned the reptile to the recesses of his sleeve, then turned away from me and withdrew. Only now did I realise that he was a small man, his diminutive frame dwarfed by the three Romans.

'Escort our charming friend to the garrison,' ordered the tall man.

The defeated tribesman left my workshop with two blades aimed at his back.

I don't think I have ever been quite so grateful to see one of my mother-in-law's premonitions come to pass.

The interloper wore a red, long-sleeved tunic and a broad military belt with a buckle of lustrous silver. Having sheathed his blade, he walked across the workshop towards me. It was normally centurions that wore red but this man carried no helmet or armour.

'It seems I timed my visit well. Who was that?'

'I don't know his name. I believe he was sent by an enemy of mine.'

'Really? Well, give me the enemy's name and I'll do what I can to ensure he never troubles you again. You are Zosimos, the renowned maker of gold?'

'I am, sir.'

'That is a relief.' The Roman leant back against a table and folded his arms across his chest. 'I have spent the last week sailing up the Nile, the week before that crossing from the capital. I work for a man who works for the Emperor. Some idiotic governor in Pannonia has signed a peace treaty with a tribe of barbarians. We need the treaty to hold but he promised them a thousand pounds of gold and, well, I gather there's currently little to spare. I understand that you can produce something that looks genuine but is less expensive?'

I was only now beginning to recover from my scare and here was another odd turn of events.

'I must thank you for your intervention, sir, but you should know that I am very busy with my work for the temple.'

'Fear not; I will ensure the priests are properly compensated. But we do need this stuff quickly. I have chartered a ship and would like to get it back to Rome with all possible haste.'

My goodwill towards the interloper was fading. His request would involve a huge amount of organisation and work. Then again, if he really was in Panopolis on behalf of the Emperor, what choice did I have?

'I mean, we wouldn't want to disappoint the Emperor, would we?'

There was only one answer to that. 'No.'

The Roman wandered towards the furnace and tapped the sheet of bronze with a knuckle. 'I mean, between you and me, it doesn't have to be top quality.' He smiled. 'Just good enough to fool a barbarian.'

Interview with Nick Brown

Can you tell us a bit about yourself? How long have you been writing and what other jobs have you had?

I've been writing seriously since 2010 but had always dabbled before that. I worked for ten years as a history and English teacher which at least offered good holidays for some valuable writing time. These days I'm a freelance writer, working on novels, screenplays and games. I've ghosted several books and scripts for clients.

What is it about Rome that inspires you?

I think it's a perfect setting for historical fiction because we know just enough to approximate most aspects of ancient life. Better still, there are endless momentous events to weave stories around. In modern, globalised, 2019 it's exciting to think of the ancient world, where so much was still a mystery and daily concerns were very different.

What inspired you to write this particular story?

I wanted to avoid my usual genre (action/adventure) and I've always been interested in alchemy. Also, Egypt is an exotic, compelling setting that I wanted to explore. I should also mention 'Becoming Gold' by Dr. Shannon Grimes – the central text I used for this short story.

Can you tell us about your other work inspired by Rome?

My 'Agent of Rome' series began with 'The Siege' in 2011 and five books have followed. I'm currently working on the seventh, and final story, 'The Last Battle.' I've also released three short stories set in the 3rd century.

What do you enjoy most about writing?

Finishing!

I think all aspects have their plusses and minuses. I usually enjoy research and plotting more than the actual writing. Editing and polishing can be very satisfying though I'm still not sure I enjoy it!

If you were transported back to the time your story is set, who is the first person you would want to talk to and why?
I would always go straight to the emperor of the time – just to observe how power was truly wielded.

What would you bring back from ancient Rome with you?
Now there's an interesting question – probably a nice silk tunic with a sliver belt buckle!

If there was one event in the period you could witness (in perfect safety) what would it be?
It has to be the early first century in Judea – I'd just really like to know!

Why do you think readers are still so thirsty for stories from this period?
Many readers are interested in how humans lived in previous eras. As authors, all we can do is create our own imagined version of the past but it's always a fascinating experiment. Life was so very different; we can include ideas, attitudes, beliefs and experiences which are utterly alien to us now.

What are you writing at the moment?
I'm working on a book for a client and two computer games as well as the last 'Agent of Rome'.

How important is it for you to be part of a community of writers, and why?
Very important. Writers are still a fairly rare breed so you're unlikely to meet many without seeking them out. I'm glad to say I've become friends with many writers in recent years through social media and organisations like the HWA. It's really helpful to hear news, compare notes and support each other's work. As with any serious career, its only really fellow

professionals that understand the realities. Generally, writers are a very supportive bunch.

Where can readers find out more about your books?
Website: nickbrownauthor.com
Facebook: Nick Brown-Agent of Rome
Twitter: @randomrome

Eagles in the Desert - Gordon Doherty

A prequel to the Legionary series

360 AD, Bezabde, The Roman-Persian Frontier....

The River Tigris sparkled in the blistering morning sun, wending like a great teal ribbon through an ancient land of dunes, dust and golden rocks. Searing emptiness stretched for miles in almost every direction. Alone in this wilderness stood the Roman border citadel of Bezabde, a loam-coloured fortress perched upon a low scarp mound, guarding the river's western banks. Up on the circular roof of the southeastern corner turret, two legionaries of the Second Parthica rested their weight on their spears and shields – painted blood-red, emblazoned with golden centaurs. Their ridge-topped helms and ring mail shirts glittered like jewels in the sunlight.

Falco listened to the playful babble of the water, and every so often he caught a trace of the damp-silt scent rising from the river's edge. A glorious contrast to the desert's dry, dusty odour. These simple things took him away from this place, from the dust and sand, from the chimeral infinity on every horizon, from all the warnings about what was out there and coming this way. For a glorious moment he sank into the welcome halls of memory, his hawk-like face spreading in a half-smile.

Arius noticed and gave him an arch look. 'What's that strange thing on your face? You've done nothing but sulk for the last month!'

'I'm thinking about home,' Falco said with a fond sigh. 'About the last time I took my boy, Pavo, fishing.' There was something about the word *last* that caused the conversation to fall into a short lull. Both men avoided each other's gaze, choosing to look out over the sands again. 'We would walk through the wards of Constantinople,' Falco eventually resumed, 'buy hot loaves and a pot of honey from the bread market at the Forum of Constantine, then leave through the Adrianople Gate. I'd give Pavo some coins to buy fruit from the smallholdings outside the city walls. Strawberries... he loves strawberries. Just a mile up the Golden Horn there is a pleasant bay – a sickle of white sand edged with smooth rocks. We'd fish for mackerel there, watching the dolphins leaping further out, feeling the hot summer wind in our hair and the sun on our faces.' He took off his helm as he spoke, cupping it underarm and letting his loose chestnut locks catch a little of the desert breeze. He closed his eyes and, for just a trice, it felt like he was truly home and with young Pavo.

The anxious wails of a baby pulled Falco from his thoughts. He looked over his shoulder into Bezabde's interior. Palms sprouted here and there amidst the warren of mud brick and marble homes. Green vines tumbled lazily from rooftop gardens. Vibrant fabrics and silks still hung in the market ward – and when they fluttered in the occasional desert breeze, it often tricked the eye, making one think there were local people there, going about their daily business. But there were no citizens at the market, and none in the streets either. Those who had not fled the city were now barricaded inside their homes, fearing what was to come. He caught sight of a gaunt mother and the crying babe in the window of a nearby terraced home. *Gods be with you*, she mouthed at him. There were others too, all looking out with that same fearful mien. The emperor had declared that Bezabde had to be defended for the glory of Rome and that the Persians had to be repelled to maintain the empire's status. But Falco knew why he stood here on the walls: for the mothers, the children, for those here who could not defend themselves. Reassured, he made to turn his eyes back to the desert outside, when he noticed something odd. A figure standing on a flat rooftop. An old woman, hunched, white-haired. She was blind, he reckoned, going by her eyes – like milky orbs. It was strange that she was up there in the open and not huddled away like the others. Stranger still was the way her blind eyes seemed to be trained... upon him.

Unnerved, he switched his gaze to the city's outer wards, where steel flashed and blinked every so often. The three legions sent here to defend the place were at work along the fortifications, in the open squares and on strategic rooftops. Furthest away, in the city's western forum, the Second Armenian Legion were but a distant glimmer, and so thinly spread upon the battlements there. A band of Zabdiceni desert archers were busy at the practice range near those western ramparts, loosing arrow after arrow into painted targets. Two days ago, these dark-skinned local tribesmen had poured into the city in support of the imperial defence. A welcome reinforcement.

In the city's central wards, horsemen from the Second Flavian Legion cantered to and fro, carrying scrolls, capes flailing in their wake as they relayed instructions to each part of the northern and western walls from *Magister Militum* Sabinianus – the commander of the defence, stationed in the palace at the heart of the city where he had set up a war room.

'Must be a fine thing to fight a battle from a couch,' Arius grunted, eyeing the palace. 'In the eight days since we got here, that fat bastard has never once set foot outside until the coolness of night, and even then it's only to ride the two streets to the wine house.'

'Aye, Generals make wars,' Falco mused wryly, 'then leave their soldiers to wage them.' As he said this, his gaze fell down to the nearby southern drill compound, where his and Arius' own Second Parthica comrades were busy sharpening their *spatha* blades, polishing their armour and the famous Parthica eagle standard, all to the tune of their chief centurion's hectoring cries. A proud legion... but a thin reserve for these southern walls, Falco thought. His eyes slid down to the stonework under his boots. This southeastern corner turret was thought a secret weak-spot – for the scarp mound was less steep here, though that much was not obvious to one looking upon the city from outside. More, the stonework was badly in need of repair. He stamped his feet on the pale flagstones as if testing their soundness. *If the Persian storm hits here...* he mused darkly.

'The chaplain asked me why us Parthica men were so uneasy,' Arius said, reading Falco's disquiet. 'I told him it was because we were not sure of this section of the defences. He said God would strengthen the rocks under our feet.'

Falco barked once with laughter. 'The Christian Priest? He's a sly one – I don't trust a word that passes his lips. You may as well have spoken to a desert hound. Put your hopes in *Mithras*, old friend. The God of the Soldiers will see us right.'

'Pah!' Arius swept a hand in the air. 'I'll bet you a skin of wine that-'

The rest of his sentence died, crushed under a distant *boom!* that burst across the land from the southern horizon, shaking Bezabde then dying with a strange crackle. Falco and Arius looked at one another, then looked south, faces draining of colour. *Boom!* the noise came again. For all the world Falco wished it was just faraway thunder, but he knew, to his marrow, that it was in fact the sound of Persian war drums. He slowly lifted his helm from the parapet and place it back on his head. As he tied his chin strap, annoyed by the trembling of his fingers, his mouth drained of moisture. All the while his eyes stared, unblinking, at the south. Nothing. Then… the heat haze flickered and a silvery dot appeared like a needle piercing through cloth, before slowly widening to fill the horizon. Now the drums throbbed in an eager rhythm. *Boom! Boom! Boom!*

Clang! A bell tolled from Bezabde's streets in a weak riposte. 'To the walls!' A tribunus bellowed in between peals. Roman horns blared from every ward in the city. Behind him, the yells of officers rose in a clamour. Men shouted, footsteps clattered on flagstones and hooves clopped – now at a gallop. Falco heard the clap of many shutters in the terrace behind him closing over and the thick, heavy clunk of timber locking bars slotting into bronze brackets as the city's four gatehouses were secured. He shot a look backwards. The streets were bare apart from the centuries of soldiers in the city's inner parts streaming towards the walls. Oddly, the blind old woman was still there on the nearby rooftop, silent… watching.

The drumming of boots intensified, then a score of legionaries rose onto the curtain wall either side of Falco's corner turret, filing along the battlements, one legionary for every crenel-gap. Three more rose onto the turret roof to reinforce Falco and

Arius, bringing with them the odour of sweat and half-eaten wheat porridge. Slaves scurried along the walls, bringing bundles of *spiculae* javelins and leather buckets of slingshot. Some brought burning braziers too, and a few man-sized spherical cages of dried willow. Artillery crews hobbled up the stony steps of the city's eight gate turrets, taking bundles of iron-headed bolts to the *ballistae* perched up there – the bolt-throwers resembling great iron eagles, beaks pointing proudly at the desert. The Zabdiceni archers split into small groups, each assigned to a turret. A squadron of six arrived beside Falco and Arius, each man with two quivers strapped to their back in an X shape. They jabbered in their desert tongue, staring south. Falco and Arius had only learned a few words of their tongue, but they needed no translator when the tribesmen wailed 'The *Shahanshah* is coming. The King of Kings is here!'

Falco and Arius watched in silence as the silvery mass on the horizon drew to within a mile of Bezabde in a bull-horn formation, casting up a huge wall of dust in its wake. Even the rumours had not predicted such might. The *Savaran* cavalry, Shahanshah Shapur's finest, seemed to stretch for miles: lancers, mounted upon tall, strong warhorses, the riders wearing jackets of iron scale and pointed helms topped with jostling, balled plumes. Either side of the mighty cavalry wing marched two vast infantry divisions: a sea of spear tips, wicker screens, headscarves and bronze, leather and iron helms. Each unit within carried a *drafsh* banner – poles draped with vibrant sheets of red, green, gold and blue depicting bears, deer, asps and lions, fluttering like the sails of ships on this silvery tide. Last to slip from the heat haze was a line of colossal creatures, the likes of which Falco had never before set eyes upon; beasts with swishing, armour-plated trunks, bronze-coated tusks and archer-packed cabins strapped to their broad backs. The elephants trumpeted angrily in the gaps between the drumbeats. At the heart of all this, Zoroastrian Magi carried the most magnificent *drafsh kavian* banner – tall as a tree – topped with a gold effigy of a soaring guardian angel, half-eagle, half-man.

Falco tried to dampen his lips with his tongue but found that it was stuck to the roof of his mouth. How many Persians were out there? Forty thousand? More? He cast a look back around Bezabde's walls. These three legions and the local archers numbered no more than six thousand. Yet even as he tried to make the imbalance seem less absurd, the Persian army wrapped around Bezabde like a strangler's hands. He noticed how they brought hundreds of ladders and artillery too – stone-throwers, wooden war-towers and rams. One ram was enormous, with a bronze beak and a pitched defensive roof, and required a team of over one hundred sweating and shackled slaves to move it. Now, faint shadows passed over the land. Falco knew without looking up that it was not cloud but carrion birds, coming to see what treats might be left come the end of the day.

'But damn,' Arius said rocking on the balls of his feet. 'My mouth is dry as sand and my bladder has swollen to the size of a watermelon. Why does it always happen on the cusp of battle?'

'Ah, the old "Soldier's Curse",' Falco said, trying to sound relaxed but failing. He noticed how Arius' eyes were trained on the giant ram, but every so often he would glance down at the stonework under their feet. 'Don't worry: look where that monstrosity is headed – to the western walls. The scarp is steep there and the walls strong. It will never make it up there.'

Even as he said this, he felt a cold hand grip and twist his guts. How, how could they prevail today? He thought of little Pavo, and suddenly felt like a fool for having left the boy on his own. With a shaking hand, he lifted one of the leather twines hanging round his neck. From it hung a bronze *phalera* – a thin bronze disc issued as a military reward, smaller than a coin. He had earned it after a battle against the Marcomanni in the distant northern woods. Embossed text ran around the edge: *Legio II Parthica*, it read. He stretched his arm out towards Arius.

'Take it,' he said.

Arius frowned. 'Why? You earned it. They called you a fool when you charged and a hero when your charge won the day!'

'If I die here,' Falco said quietly so the men nearby wouldn't hear, 'then Pavo will have nobody.' He stopped, gulping, achingly sad for the past, for the days just before his son's birth, the last few times he had held his wife. It had been a traumatic labour, but a blessing that at least Pavo had survived. 'Take this. If you make it through this and I don't – get this to him. There is so much I should have told him, so much he needs to know. At the very least I want him to know that I was thinking about him… at the last.'

Arius looked haunted for a moment, then he forced a comrade's smile and snatched the phalera. 'You always get maudlin before battle,' he said with a gruff chuckle. 'Those skins of wine we set aside for later, I'll bet you mine we're both still alive to enjoy them come dusk tonight, and I'll be giving you this back.'

Falco returned his grin. It was the soldier's way, to mask white-hot fear behind humour.

Just then, the Persian lines halted in a thick ring around the city, and the thunder of drums stopped. Silence bar the hot breeze, the croak of cicadas and the shuffling and snorting of horses. A small party rolled forth: a quartet of ironclad and masked *pushtigban* royal guardsmen carrying a rush throne, the backrest a panoply of peacock feathers. Shapur, King of Kings, sat upon it, draped in saffron and purple robes, soft calfskin slippers and a tall, purple hat. His magnificent beard and long hair hung in dark, oiled curls across his chest and shoulders. A sweating, bare-chested and shaven-headed lackey moved out before the enemy king, stopped and addressed the walls. 'Citizens and soldiers of Bezabde, rejoice!' he cried. 'You should be honoured, for you are in the presence of greatness. Shapur, the Conqueror of Nations, the King of Kings, the lord of all Persia… is here! Feast your eyes on his mighty war machine. Ask yourself: is it not fitting that you should bow down to him and submit to his greatness? Do you not know of his magnanimity? So I intreat you, Romans, throw open your gates, come forth, give Bezabde to its rightful owner, and in return you can enjoy… his mercy.'

A horrible silence hung in the air. Falco and Arius looked at one another. Both had heard tales of this 'mercy': entire cohorts of captured legionaries buried to their necks in the sand and left there for their skulls to bake in the desert heat; wretches pierced

19

through the shoulder and linked together through those festering holes with chains, driven like cattle to work in the foul underground salt mines; and Valerian, an Emperor of Rome who, some one hundred years ago had been captured out in these parts – rumour was he had been kept alive for years, used as a footstool for the Shahanshah to step upon when mounting his horse, before finally the King of Kings became bored of his toy and had Valerian peeled of his skin. Falco heard some distant squabbling from the heart of the city – the sound of that irritating chaplain's voice, arguing in favour of the terms. But not a soul within Bezabde moved to open the gates.

'Very well,' the sweaty Persian orator said after a short wait and a conference with his master.

Shapur was carried backwards, into the shade of a grand pavilion tent. Just before he slipped from view, he clapped his hands once.

In response to this, a coal-skinned *mahout* elephant rider, naked bar a cape and a loincloth and with bulbous weights hanging from his earlobes, read this signal. He stood up on the elephant's neck, put a giant ibex horn to his lips, tilted his head back and let his chest swell with breath. A horrible, baritone moan crawled across the land, infiltrating every space within Bezabde. The moan rose suddenly into a high-pitched eerie wail. Then, with a mighty cry and a thunder of boots, hooves and wheels, the Persian war machine burst into life. Dust rose from every direction as the noose around Bezabde began to contract. Falco saw a great mass of infantry – one of the four armies out there – coming for their section. War towers, ladders, spears and curved *shamshir* swords swished and glinted and the many soldiers howled and chanted.

'Be ready,' Falco shouted over the din, attempting to fortify the hearts of the small knot of men up here with him. He was not an officer, but he was more experienced than most of the legionaries with him. He braced near one crenel-gap, using his shield to fill it, levelling the tip of his spear near the top. Arius did likewise by his left. But he saw the three other legionaries on the turret trembling, teeth chattering. One's face was wet with tears pouring from wide eyes.

'How long have we fought alongside one another? How long?' Falco bawled at the three. 'We have faced forest tribes in the north who outnumbered us like ants. Did we not spend that night by the fire, toasting a great victory? Drusus,' he called to the tearful one, 'you fought using the eagle standard in place of a spear or a sword. You were like an animal, sweeping the enemy away in droves. Pulso, it was you – *you* – who matched the tribal chief in combat and knocked him to his knees. Latro, you gave chase alone to ride down the enemy scouts who sped away to rouse reinforcements – had you not we would have been overwhelmed by them. All of you, you have proved yourself before. Do not fear the swarming hawks out there – for we… we are *eagles!* And each of us is worth one hundred of them.'

Pulso straightened up, Drusus wiped his face and turned a rictus-glare out upon the advancing enemy, Latro falling into a similar stance beside him. Reassured, Falco turned his attentions back to the wall of Persians rumbling closer and closer. Only two hundred paces away. The Zabdiceni archers behind him began showering a thin rain of shafts down at the enemy front. A few dozen enemy were struck, shafts plunging into their eye sockets, necks and shoulders. Puffs and gouts of blood shot up and these stricken ones halted as if they had forgotten something, before they sank from sight. In reply, a storm of enemy arrows, slingshot and javelins clattered and whacked against the parapets. Chunks of pale stone flew in every direction, dust exploded in choking bursts, Falco's shield bucked and shuddered as scores of missiles battered against it. Arius yelped as a javelin skated from the tip of his helm, denting the fin-ridge.

'Hold steady,' Falco bellowed, seeing that all along the walls, just a handful of legionaries had fallen, peppered with arrows, crumpling where they stood or folding over the parapet. The thin Roman defence was weathering this opening storm well. But then he heard a groan of timber and strained ropes. He saw the catapults amidst the Persian lines buck, shudder and settle, saw something whoosh through the air towards the walls. With a great crash and an explosion of dust and thrown rocks, almost a score of legionaries by the southern gatehouse were cast backwards like toys, screaming, one man half-torn at the waist, his guts trailing behind him like wet, red ribbons. More catapults loosed. *Crash!* Another section of the wall top ripped away.

Falco saw the men beside him pale with shock. Now he was lost for words. Worse, he spotted the fleet of smaller rams rolling proud of the closing Persian noose, being guided up the scarp near the beset southern gatehouse. The rams were little more than sharpened pine trunks housed under protective roofs of hide and wicker, being pushed forward by teams of twelve. In response, the two ballistae on the gatehouse turret tilted, bucked and spat forth a pair of great iron bolts. These, aimed at the foremost ram, ripped it to shreds, tearing through the protective roof and skewering three of the team through their chests. But the other rams rolled on up the slope, closer to the walls. Roman *spiculae* and arrows poured down on these ones, but these missiles were too light to penetrate the defensive roofs. The first ram reached and struck the base of the southern defences, sending a stark shudder around the entire circuit of the curtain wall, so much so that the merlons against which Falco was braced shivered madly. The second ram smashed against the bronze-banded southern gates. The third and fourth too – a rapid assault.

'Bring the urns!' an officer cried from the battlements above the beset gates.

An acrid stink floated through the baking air. Pitch, Falco realised, shooting a look along the defences to see the men there heaving great urns of boiling black liquid. Others carried buckets of glowing sand – heated in the city kilns and so hot they could only carry the buckets on poles. In one graceless heave, they emptied the contents of these vessels down upon the rams. Falco witnessed the fate of one of the ram squadrons. The leather-armoured man at the head of the device was doubled over as he worked the ram, but when glowing sand hit him like a sudden shower, he stood bolt upright and unleashed the most inhuman scream, clawing at his face, wrenching at his armour where the sand had slid inside to burn like brands all across his torso. Worse for the ones who were doused with the bubbling pitch – they fell and rolled, coated in the unctuous filth. One man sat up on his knees, hands outspread, the skin on his face sloughing away like well-cooked meat from a bone. Zabdiceni archers loosed fire arrows into this sweltering chaos and, vitally, every one of the smaller rams went up in flames. The crews fled, some ablaze and flailing like human torches. The defenders cheered, but within a heartbeat, the commander, the fire archers and the men who had brought the buckets and urns to the walls disappeared in an explosion of rock and dust as another catapult rock struck home. When the dust began to clear, all that was left was a crazy pattern of red blotches, limbs and crushed armour. Runnels of blood rolled down the stonework towards the broken rams – a crumpled heap of burning wreckage and smoking bodies.

'Falco – they're almost upon us!' Arius wailed.

Falco twisted away from the horrible scene at the southern gates and peered over the rim of his shield. The infantry mass coming for their turret were but a hundred paces away now. He could see the bulging whites of the enemy eyes, the feral sneers, the sharpness of their blades. Fearsome Median spearmen, Kurdish javelin brigades, masses of *paighan* – lightly armed but fanatical fighters. They surged up the low scarp, closer, closer, ladders held overhead. Behind them a high war tower rocked and swayed, the man perched on top of the timber device shouting to the ones steering it down on the ground.

Falco knew which order he had to give. The words rose onto his tongue and they tasted like ashes. But they *had* to be spoken. For the mothers and children within the city. For little Pavo, back in Constantinople. 'Ignite!' he called to the Zabdiceni men behind him. He heard the striking of flint hooks, smelt the tang of smoke, saw the orange glow rise behind him.

'Ready,' they barked.

As one, Falco, Arius and the other three legionaries guarding the turret top stepped back. The Zabdiceni six rushed to fill those spots, three pairs each carrying one of the wicker balls, now ablaze, on the ends of poles. With a jerk of the poles they sent the blazing orbs toppling over the wall's edge. The three fiery cages bounced on the scarp, dust puffing up, then rolled towards the upcoming Persian infantry mass. Persian attackers scrambled and fell as they tried to get out of the way, parting like the waters of a river hitting three piers of a bridge. But two of the fiery spheres plunged into the Persian ranks before the men down there could get out of the way, bowling dozens from their feet, searing others, setting light to the clothing of more. The stink of smoke now became streaked with the stench of burning meat and hair. The Persian mass on the slope swirled and staggered. Eighty or so had fallen – the rest were dazed, delayed, but not for long.

'Archers, step back. Legionaries, back to your defensive positions,' Falco brayed to the few legionaries, waving them back towards the crenelations. He had taken but one step in that direction when he heard the buck and shudder of a catapult somewhere outside. A heartbeat later, the world before him burst in a golden storm and a thunderous boom, throwing him backwards in a gale of blinding grit and a thick rain of something wet. For a moment he was lost, confused, deafened, blinking, his face coated in dust and... blood? *Where are the archers?* he mouthed, staring at the spot on the turret's edge where the Zabdiceni six had been. They were gone. The crenelations too. The ramshackle turret had withstood the strike, but, like a boxer whose front teeth have been punched out, the stretch of turret top facing the Persian siege was a ragged, wide gap. From the corner of his eye he saw the strips of skin and smears of red, all that remained of the poor Zabdiceni six.

His head pounded with shock, staring at the strange wooden shapes appearing all along the broken edge of the defences. Now his hearing returned. *Clack, clack, clack,* more ladders swung up to rest against the ruined section of parapet. The same noise rang out all around Bezabde's fortifications.

Falco staggered over to the smashed section of turret defences and stared down the array of ladders, seeing myriad twisted, baleful faces glaring back as they scrambled upwards like spiders, dripping with steel. He felt Arius arrive by his side. 'Fill the gap!' Arius howled to the other three stunned, dust-coated legionaries. The three shambled over and helped form a basic line – just wide enough to plug the shattered section of parapet like human merlons.

A Persian champion with bloodshot eyes and a feral look led the way, surging up the central ladder, others competing to beat him to the top.

'*Ready!*' Falco bawled. The champion drew a shamshir from his back-scabbard, bounding up the last few steps of the ladder one-handed, swinging the blade for a low strike at Falco's legs. Falco dropped his shield just as the strike came. The shamshir bit deep into the leather and wood, sending splinters flying. The champion's rictus became a wicked grin... until he tried to withdraw the sword, and realised it was stuck. Falco braced his body, lifted his spear overhand and lanced downwards, sending the tip plunging into the man's shoulder, deep into his chest. A gout of blood pumped into the air and a light mist of it wafted over Falco's helm, face and shoulders, the metallic stink unbearable. Falco wrenched his spear back and the foe fell away from the ladder, his face now blank and lost. The falling corpse caused Falco's mind to flash with a thousand imaginings. What had he done? Who had he killed? A man. A father? A husband? A son? Remorse rose within him like a whip of fire. It was the bane that every legionary – every soldier – endured, yet few spoke of. In rapid succession, he speared again and again, two more swift deaths. Either side of him Arius and the other three worked in the same way, arms jerking, spears punching down. Within moments, the stonework of the turret was glistening with blood.

A shrill scream sounded when one climbing Persian grabbed Latro's shin, hauling him from his place at the turret's broken edge. The Roman fell in a flurry of thrashing limbs, landing on the scarp below with a *whump* of many breaking bones and a star of redness. Falco stared at the corpse numbly. A military brother of many years, gone in a heartbeat.

From the corner of his eye he saw the assault all along the southern walls, swells of Persians swarming up the ladders, two war towers reaching the defences as well – scores of enemy soldiers pouring out over the drawbridges at the tops to surge into the legionary defenders there. Flashes of steel and puffs of red rose all along the battlements. Horns blared, voices swung between proud cries and wet death screams. His spear arm grew numb as he worked. Pulso, by his side suddenly let his shield go, the screen toppling away over the drop.

'What are you doi-' Falco started, but then he saw that the legionary had somehow lost his helm and now a Persian shamshir rested in the crest of his skull, wedged deep like a knife in a block of fat. The legionary staggered and swayed, arms like limp ribbons, sword dropping too. Pulso stared at Falco, eyes wide like moons, as a soup of dark blood and pieces of brain matter sheeted down his face, before he crumpled where he stood, one arm hanging out over the drop. In Pulso's place stood the killer, who wrenched the sword free and drew back to strike at Falco. Without a moment of thought, Falco dropped into a crouch and speared up into his belly. The blow was ruinous, snapping his spear and bursting from the foe's back. The stink of torn bowels hit him like a slap as the man's blue-grey gut ropes sped free like a knot of snakes. As the foe fell to his knees, vomiting blood, Falco realised it was over. Just three legionaries left up here. Not enough to hold this turret. Not with thousands of Persians vying to climb up here and...

A shadow rose over him. The war tower rocked up like a Kraken's head emerging from the waves at a boat's edge. Falco stared at the wild-eyed man perched on the war tower roof, heard the thunderous shouts of the ones behind the closed timber drawbridge on its upper floor. With a whack of timber hitting stone, the drawbridge fell down, and a dozen Persian warriors surged across for the turret roof.

'Get back!' Falco cried to his comrades. He, Arius and Drusus retracted like claws, backstepping rapidly to come together in a tiny defensive knot near the city-edge of the turret.

'Shields, together!' Falco boomed. 'Shoulder-to-shoulder!'

The three legionaries clacked their shields into place in a mini-wall as more and more Persians poured out from the war tower and more still clambered up from the ladders and across the turret roof. They came at the trio with a shared war-cry. Spearless, he ripped his spatha from its scabbard. A spear strike came at him and he could only block with his sword, sending up a shower of sparks. When a second man swished a death-strike at Arius, he swung his blade up and into that one's armpit, saving his comrade. As they fought, he felt Arius and Drusus jolt and shudder, heard them croak and cry, grunt and swear. The stonework underfoot grew wet and slippery with blood, and he felt the Persians press ever harder upon them. Drusus died first, shield pulled away and his head staved in by a mace.

Now the Persians swamped Falco and Arius. Each was driven onto one knee in their tiny shield shell, a brutal rain of swords and spears battering at them, one ripping across Falco's bicep, another slashing his ear, a third piercing his leg near the knee.

'Mithras, hear us!' Falco cried as his shield began to dissolve like kindling.

The reply came in the form of a silvery flash and a baritone cry. Sixteen Parthica legionaries scrambled up the steps onto the turret top and crashed into the flank of the Persians. They barrelled some over, hacked many down and drove the remainder back to the ladders, bowling a few from the edge and to their deaths.

Shaking, panting, Falco and Arius lowered their shields, watching at the sixteen reinforcement legionaries used long poles to force the Persian ladders away from the walls. The tall ladders swayed and teetered as they were pushed almost vertical – each still with a handful of men mid-climb – before they toppled backwards with a chorus of wails as the higher climbers were dashed on the ground. Likewise, a storm of blazing arrows hammered into the wooden war tower docked against the turret. The great device went up like a torch, and when the men in the lower floors fled, the weight of others still in the upper floors sent it pitching over. It fell like a beaten giant, exploding on the scarp slope in a storm of timber and fire.

Falco and Arius shared a look, then rose from their knees, seeing the Persian assault being repelled like this all along the curtain wall. The Shahanshah's armies streamed back down the city scarp mound in disorder. The sixteen who had saved them had come from a section nearby where the besiegers had already been repulsed.

'We did it? We won?' Arius croaked.

The centurion amongst the sixteen reinforcements – face striped with sweat and blood – gave him a grave look. 'We repelled them, but that was just the first wave.'

Indeed, Falco noticed how the retreating Persian soldiers were merely settling back into their original siege circle. He glanced across the city's defences: the catapult-battered parapets were now like a motley collection of broken teeth, sections glistening wet with blood or draped with spear and arrow-studded bodies. Many hundreds, maybe more than two thousand legionaries dead, he estimated. Just as many Persians had perished, but that was merely a dent in their huge numbers. He stepped over close to the centurion, so nobody else would hear. 'Sir… the *first* wave? Can we weather a second?'

The centurion's mouth moved as if to rebuke him, but his lips settled into a tight line and he merely nodded. 'It will not be easy, but,' he scanned along the dusty land outside the walls, nodding to the giant bronze-beaked ram near the southwestern section, 'as long as that monstrosity stays away from this turret. We have enough men still to hold out,' the man assured him.

Falco gazed along the walls again, unconvinced. From the edges of his vision, he noticed that the strange old crone was still up on that rooftop, sentinel-like through all that had gone on. *Who are you?* he mouthed, staring back at her.

But then a cry rose from the streets. Both turned to see a messenger boy running towards the southern gatehouse from the war room at the heart of the city. 'Open the gates,' he cried. 'Magister Militum Sabinianus wants to send an envoy to the Persian siege lines.'

Falco, Arius and the centurion all bristled.

'What?' the centurion gasped.

'He's seeking terms? Has the fat bastard lost his mind?' Arius growled.

'Lost control of his bowels, more like,' Falco said, 'one sight of battle from his palace rooftop has been enough to break his famous "courage".'

A few of the nearby legionaries laughed wryly at this. But Falco's attentions had moved on, his gaze snagged by the diplomacy party Sabinianus had chosen, moving through the streets. A knot of four slaves, two legionaries and one man in a long, trailing white robe and a soldier's belt and red cloak. The chaplain.

'Set aside your fears,' the chaplain called up to the walls as he neared the gates, holding up his gold *Chi-Rho* staff. 'I will do what is right to see that this day ends well.'

Falco groaned. 'Of all the negotiators to choose…'

'Pah,' Arius croaked. 'I told you already, he said God would save us today.'

Falco gave him a wry look. 'I'd say it was our legionary brothers who did that.'

Powerless, they watched as the small party departed through the battered but intact southern gates, and trooped out to the Shahanshah's grand pavilion.

An hour passed; an hour of men sitting with their backs to the parapets where they were intact, drinking, faces burnt and blistered and caked in dust and gore. Many remained transfixed upon the Shahanshah's tent, waiting for movement or signs of agreement. A *medicus* moved around the men, tending to their wounds, bandaging Falco's gashed knee and bicep. Flies began to gather in black clouds, droning over the bloodied sections of the walls, laying eggs in the ripped bodies. Vultures too, perching on the defences, pecking and wrenching innards from corpses. One pulled and pulled at the eye of a dead man near Falco until the sinew stretched and snapped. He swished his arm to scare the bird off, then he and Arius sat to drink a full water skin each, but neither touched the hard tack or salted beef in the small ration bag a slave brought to them. Food was the furthest thing from both men's minds.

'He's done it!' one legionary called.

Falco and Arius' heads shot up, seeing almost every other defender rising to look. He and Arius stood too and saw the chaplain emerge from the Shahanshah's tent.

'He's made a bargain,' Arius whispered in relief. 'He's saved us.'

But as Falco watched, a terrible sense of something askew crept over him. The slaves and two soldiers of the Roman embassy stood in a line beside the chaplain, but their heads hung low, dejected. One by one they were forced to their knees. Next, a bare-chested brute of a man walked along the back of the line, carefully placing an iron bolt above the vertex of each skull then pounding down upon it with a hammer. Each kneeling man spasmed and blood leapt up, before the body slid to one side, twitching. Soon, only the chaplain remained.

'But... but he said God was with him,' Arius whispered. 'That he would do whatever it took to see that the day ended well.'

Falco watched as the hammer and bolt man walked behind the chaplain... then walked on by. A Persian general bedecked in bronze scale moved over to the chaplain's side. They seemed to be talking. Then, with a deliberate slowness, the chaplain raised one arm, pointing across to the city... right at the southeastern corner turret.

'He has,' Falco burred. 'He has done *exactly* what he needed to do to see that today ends well... for him.'

The Persian horns blew once more and a great wail of dismay rose from all around the Roman defences as, in the afternoon sunlight, the entire Persian force rolled forth once more, converging on Falco's turret. The gargantuan ram rocked and swayed amidst it all.

'Together,' the centurion croaked.

Falco heard the blood crash in his ears as he once again stepped over numbly to the blown-apart stretch of parapet, squaring his shoulders, holding his shield firmly, his spatha resting on the upper edge. Arius and a dozen others gathered with him, shield-to-shield, shoulder-to-shoulder, standing once more like human merlons. A handful of the men to the rear began to yammer in panic as the assault force rolled closer. Three staggered backwards, then threw down their shields and scrambled down from the walls, fleeing to the inner city, hearts and heads filled with fear.

Falco, Arius, the centurion and the others knew that same fear but stood firm, all realising that if this turret fell, then Bezabde would too.

'Remember what I told you,' Falco snarled in Arius' direction. 'Should the will of the soldier-god be thwarted today... you must get the phalera to Pavo... aye?'

'No,' Arius croaked, voice tight with battle-nerves. He stuffed the phalera into the collar of Falco's mail shirt. 'Fight... live! We can still win this day. You *will* see Pavo again!'

Falco half-laughed, half-growled, then stared along the length of his spear. 'Wine tonight, aye?'

'Aye!' Arius cackled in reply.

Boom! Boom! Boom! The Persian war drums struck up a rapid rhythm as the swells of ironclad infantry converged like a river of molten silver, rolling towards the turret and carrying hundreds of ladders. Trumpeting elephants stomped along with them, backs packed with archers. Worst of all, the huge ram cut through the midst of this tide like a galley and was first to roll up the scarp mound, leading the assault.

'Rain fire on that ram!' the centurion howled. A squadron of Zabdiceni loosed a hail of blazing missiles, but they thocked onto the vinegar and water-soaked bull-hides draped over the great device and fizzled out. Men brought fresh urns of sand and bubbling pitch, but the ram's stout roof sluiced the searing mixtures away from the men driving the device. The giant ram slowed by the foot of the turret, the top of it nearly level with the turret roof. The great ram groaned as the mighty bronze-beaked log within swung backwards. Falco, Arius and every legionary threw their spears at the device in a desperate effort to find some weakness, to sever some vital rope or break a load-bearing length of timber. But the retracted ram weathered it all.

The log whooshed back towards the turret, the bronze beak hammering into the lower stonework with a deafening crunch. Falco felt the world under him shake and shift. There was an odd moment of silence, the Persian clamour of war cries and the storm of horns and elephant roars fading in gleeful anticipation... before the turret growled like a woken bear and the flagstones under his feet shifted violently. White-hot fear rose up through him. The legionaries around him erupted in a terrified wail. With a rolling thunder of disintegrating wood and stone, the turret collapsed underneath their feet, the wretched song of destruction and screaming rolling out across skies above Bezabde.

In those moments, Falco knew chaos, falling, grievous blows to every part of his body. Crushing pain. A landing that cast the air from his lungs and the light from his mind. Half-buried, broken. With his last traces of strength he managed to clasp the phalera. Somewhere outside this tomb of rubble, he heard the triumphant cries of the Persian masses, the drums, the enemy horns, the crunch of their boots and hooves as they spilled over the remains of the fallen turret and into Bezabde. The very final sound was the most terrible of all – the panicked screams of the mothers and wailing of their babes as the pillage and slaughter began.

Come dusk, when the Persians had sacked Bezabde and gloried in their victory, when the Shahanshah had gleefully discussed what horrors he might subject the wounded and captive legionaries to, when almost all earthly senses were gone from the shell of Falco the legionary, a shadow fell over his prone, motionless form. The shadow of a withered old woman. The shadow crouched by his outstretched, scraped and dust-covered hand and took the phalera from it.

'You could have run like the others, but you chose to stand against it all,' she said respectfully. 'Pavo will know what you did here, and he too will know greatness.' With that, she rose and turned away, her shadow fading into the dusk, changing shape, rising towards the sky like a bird.

Somewhere high above, an eagle screamed. It was the sound of destiny.

Interview with Gordon Doherty

Can you tell us a bit about yourself? How long have you been writing and what other jobs have you had?

I've been writing stories since I was a nipper. It was cartoons at first then, when I was a teenager, short stories and poems and cringey 'woe-is-me' songs during university, where I studied Physics & Astronomy. Day job work (IT) took me away from such things, but only for a few years. I soon found myself using every free moment to read history and historical fiction, and both allowed my imagination to spread its wings and soar. By my mid-20s I realised I had to go back to writing. Best decision ever.

What is it about Rome that inspires you?

When I first began to read about the republic and the empire, I was struck with a great sense of loss – a simpler, more idyllic period that could never be recovered. Then, when I began to *really* delve into the history, I realised that ancient Rome was just as complex and twisted as modern life (okay, maybe without the smartphones). But the hooks were in, and in particular the later empire had me absolutely gripped. Even after years of reading about it, I still find the fall of the Roman Empire and the metamorphosis from late antiquity into the 'Dark Ages' absolutely fascinating. To think of how it must have been for the people living through that seismic transition – the conflict, the upheaval, the pride and refusal to let the past slip away – just spirits me away every time.

What inspired you to write this particular story?

There's a consistent, underlying theme that runs through all of my books - 'absent father, lost son'. The Legionary series opens with a young, orphaned Pavo being sold off in a slave market, and his struggle is as much about becoming a man without fatherly guidance as it is about becoming a legionary. This prequel 'Eagles in the Desert' allowed me to instead live out the experience of Falco (Pavo's father), during the great siege from which he never returned home. It allowed me to consider the emotions from the other side of the fence: the regrets, the guilt, the coming to terms with it all. Also – and on a slightly lighter note – it allowed me to dive right into a really violent and energetic siege – swords, blood, heads flying everywhere!

If there was one event in the period you could witness (in perfect safety) what would it be?

The Trojan War. I think it's safe to say that there *was* some major conflict between the Mycenaean Greeks and the Trojans sometime near the end of the Bronze Age. But all we have is oral tradition, stitching together mythology and legend and precious fragments of fact. While we know lots about later periods of history, this era has always felt like a gold mine to me. In fact, I once wrote a time travel short story about going back to witness it all.

What are you writing at the moment?

Ha! Speaking of the Bronze Age, I've just this summer launched a brand new series set in in the 14th & 13th c B.C. 'Empires of Bronze' kicks off a few decades before the Trojan War, and follows the Hittite Empire – of whom Troy was a loyal vassal state – in their struggles against the mighty contemporary powers of Egypt, Assyria and the Mycenaeans. This project has indeed been a revelation, an absolute treasure trove of a time period to work with. They don't refer to the end of that era as 'The Bronze Age Collapse' for nothing! Book 1 of this saga 'Empires of Bronze: Son of Ishtar' is out now: http://getbook.at/eob1

Where can readers find out more about your books?

My website: www.gordondoherty.co.uk – where you can sign up for my newsletter

Facebook: GordonDohertyAuthor

Twitter: @GordonDoherty

Alter Ego - Ruth Downie

As far as Gaius Petreius Ruso was concerned, there were three things that were best avoided on a long journey.

The first was any large expanse of water, although as Britannia was an island, some hours of lurching and pitching and praying for it to be over had been inevitable.

The second was women. In truth women were best avoided at any time, since he annoyed them. This echo of his ex-wife's voice remained with him even though her physical presence had packed its bags and gone back to live with her father well over a year ago. There had been a brief time since then when he thought he might prove Claudia wrong with a woman who didn't seem to find him in any way annoying—but that was before the woman's husband caught her with the chief centurion, and Ruso knew now that he'd had a lucky escape.

The third thing to avoid was revealing what was inside the bag that he always carried with him. Once they knew, people felt the need to tell him things. Some wanted to tell him what a waste of time doctors were. Others decided that he would find their symptoms as interesting as they did themselves. He had recently been forced to spend three days in a hot carriage with a cloth merchant who not only delivered daily reports on his cough, but regularly saved what it brought up and offered it for Ruso's inspection.

Thus, on safely reaching the nearest shore of Britannia, Ruso had left his bulkier luggage to sail around the coast without him, and set off to ride north with only the bag and a change of clothing. Anyone who asked about his future role with the Legion rapidly lost interest when he said, "Administration."

All had gone well for the first few days out of Londinium. Even the British weather was drier than he had been led to expect. But last night a couple of tribunes had arrived at the posting-station, and this morning all the decent horses had been commandeered to be sat upon by more important military backsides than his own. Standing in the early morning chill of the stable yard, Ruso gazed at the hairy legs of the hollow-faced mare on offer.

When he failed to reply to, "She won't give you any bother, boss," the ostler tried, "She always stands like that."

"Hm." Ruso doubted that a horse who insisted on resting one front leg when stationary would get him over the horizon, let alone all the way to the next posting-station north.

"Still a place in the carriage, sir!" called a voice. Ruso glanced at the mare, and at the covered vehicle waiting in the gateway. Then he looked up at the grey clouds of an indecisive British sky, and made his choice.

He regretted it immediately. A man who is uneasy in female company does not want to find that the only remaining seat in a confined space is opposite two cheery young women who are offering greetings in guttural Latin and gesturing to him to sit. Ruso did the only thing he could do in the circumstances: he acknowledged his fellow-passengers with a polite nod, crammed his medical bag in under the seat, and pretended to fall asleep.

He could not, of course, actually go to sleep. The slightest loss of concentration might combine with a deep pot-hole to send him pitching head-first into the lap of one or other of the young women. Ruso resigned himself to jolting up and down for the next few hours with his legs braced and his eyes shut. A position which, as he rapidly discovered, had distressing similarities to being on board a ship.

Several grim days—or possibly two or three hours—later, they stopped at a roadside stall to buy drinks, stretch their legs and visit the latrine: a shack over a long plank with holes at regular intervals.

The young women, chatting in a tongue Ruso didn't recognise, settled themselves at the table outside the stall and sent their heavily-muscled slave to fetch refreshments. Meanwhile Ruso spotted the driver unloading the luggage of a passenger who had been sitting farther forward, and hurried to take the departing man's place. He was now facing a plaid-trousered, wild-haired Briton. The Briton smelled faintly of sheep, but the opening in the front wall of the carriage allowed fresh air to waft in and also allowed Ruso to peer out and watch the moist greenness of Britannia rolling towards them.

His place opposite the women was filled by a bulky young man who, once his considerable amount of luggage had been stowed on the baggage cart behind them, seemed eager to demonstrate all the sociability that Ruso lacked.

Even before they had rumbled past the stand of trees on the horizon, the entire carriage had learned that the new man was Lucius Ateius Capito, an officer on his way to a posting that he wasn't allowed to talk about. The young women introduced themselves as two sisters whose widowed father had recently died. One—the blonde one, Ruso thought, although he was not going to look round and check—was Laelia, the smaller darker one Annia. They were travelling from their home province to a fort on the border, where their brother was a centurion. They had never made a trip on their own before. It was very exciting. No, they did not think they were especially brave. In fact at times they were a little nervous, but they had their slave with them to look after them. Yes, they were finding Britannia very interesting. Although yes, it was a little wild. They were looking forward to seeing their brother.

Undeterred by having exhausted all the usual topics of conversation in the first five hundred paces, Capito moved on to offering advice. About travel, about Britannia, about anything else that crossed his mind - apart, of course, from the posting he wasn't allowed to discuss.

The women's responses of "Really?" and "Oh, that's very interesting!" and "I did not know that!" sounded genuinely encouraging. Ruso carried on half-listening in the hope of learning something useful. He knew almost nothing of what lay ahead. The colleague who had urged him to seek a posting here had assured him that Britannia was at the forefront of something or other - although gazing out at the goats and unkempt small boys and overburdened pedlars shambling along beside the road, it was hard to remember what.

According to Capito, the problem with the Britons was not that they were unintelligent, but that they were intractably difficult and quarrelsome. "The ones in the south have settled down quite nicely now," he told his admiring audience, "but the further north you go, the more argumentative they get. And the more hills there are for them to hide in."

The Briton opposite Ruso carried on gazing at the holes in his boots, oblivious to this assessment of his countrymen in a foreign tongue.

"…which makes them something of a nuisance to deal with," continued Capito. "I'm sure your brother will have found the same thing."

"Oh dear!" said one of the young women. "Do you think we will be safe on the border?"

It had taken Ruso a long time to learn that the wisest response whenever Claudia asked his opinion was not to offer it, but instead to find out what she thought and agree with her. Capito, however, marched on without bothering to scout ahead. "You'll be perfectly safe in the fort," he declared, "but you should ask your brother's advice about the streets outside, and don't travel anywhere else without an escort. Oh, and one more word of advice…" He lowered his voice from the pitch required for a speech to the Senate to that suitable for a local council meeting. "That necklace. I'd keep it hidden if I were you. You never know who's watching. There are natives all over the place, and they talk to each other."

Ruso closed his eyes and wished he could close his ears. He must finally have slept, because when he awoke even Capito seemed to have run out of things to say and the carriage was lurching in through the gateway of the official accommodation at Bannaventa.

He was stepping down to join the other weary passengers in the cobbled yard when a voice murmured in his ear, "I hope you didn't find me too much of a nuisance to deal with."

Ruso swung round. There was no-one remaining in the carriage but the wild-haired Briton who smelled of sheep. "You could have told him to shut up," Ruso said. "Nobody would have minded."

"I was enjoying it." The native's Latin was perfect despite a strong regional accent. "It's good to hear that we're not unintelligent."

39

Before Ruso could reply, the man strode past him toward the open gateway and was gone. As was another of Ruso's preconceptions about Britannia.

Capito's travel pass, as befitted a man on a secret mission, was of a higher order than Ruso's, and entitled him to his own personal room in the inn. He departed to it only after assuring the two women that he would see them at dinner. While the civilian travellers waited to pay the bald-headed innkeeper for their beds, Ruso was assigned a modest space in a shared room. He deposited his cloak, had a brief wash and headed for the bar in the hope of getting through a meal before Capito had finished unpacking.

He almost succeeded: he was just wiping the last smears of beef stew out of his bowl with a chunk of bread when a familiar voice boomed down the corridor. Capito was escorting his new lady friends to the bar, perhaps because there were indeed natives all over the place. One of them was now approaching Ruso with the wine-jug and offering him a refill.

Ruso shook his head. "Early night." He washed the bread down with the last mouthful from his cup before heading across the darkening yard to the stables. The ostler promised to see what he could do about finding him a decent horse for tomorrow. Ruso, who had no spare cash for a bribe, thanked him and bade him goodnight. He picked his way back over the uneven cobbles and was glad to find a lamp burning in the outhouse latrine. He was less pleased to find the muscular servant of the two women occupying the seat in the corner, bent forward and groaning softly.

Ruso settled himself as far away as possible, but the groaning was hard to ignore. Finally he said, "Are you all right?"

The man looked at him with no understanding, and Ruso realised he had never heard the women address him in anything but their native tongue.

"All right?" Ruso repeated, gesturing toward him and raising his eyebrows. He hoped he wasn't going to regret asking.

The man flapped a hand at him as if shooing away his concern, and went back to leaning forward and groaning. Ruso left him to it. Perhaps that was how they did things in whatever province these people came from.

Alone in the near-dark with several empty beds and a jumble of other men's luggage, Ruso stretched out on the straw mattress. He locked his hands behind his head and contemplated the faint lines of the slats in the bunk above him. He became aware that his jaw was clenched. His eyes were screwed up to peer at a view that was no longer there. He made a deliberate effort to relax the tight muscles in his shoulders. Deepening his breathing, he felt himself finally drifting into sleep.

If only the woman who was screaming in his dream would stop. If she didn't, she would wake him up, and—

There was shouting now as well. Men's and women's voices.

Somebody said into the darkness, "What's going on?"

Ruso's first ungracious thought was that someone had finally cracked and murdered Capito. Then he thought he ought to go and see if anyone was injured. It was all very well masquerading as a clerk, but it was hardly fair not to offer help if someone needed it. He rolled off the bunk, fumbled his way to the door and padded barefoot down the corridor in the direction of the noise.

Evidently it wasn't as late as he thought: the knot of people clustered in the entrance hall were all still fully dressed. Laelia was sobbing on her sister's shoulder. Capito towered awkwardly over both the women. The bald head of the innkeeper gleamed in the lamplight while the slaves in the background were doing what slaves did when something exciting happened: trying to look inconspicuous so nobody would think to send them away. Ruso noted with relief that the muscular one seemed to have regained his composure.

"You tried to do the right thing, sister," Annia was saying. "It is not your fault."

"Of course it's not her fault!" boomed Capito, glaring at the innkeeper. "This is outrageous!"

Laelia wailed, "He'll be so angry with me!"

"He will not be angry with you," her sister promised. "He will be angry with the thief."

"Quite right too!" put in Capito.

"But I was such a fool!

"Not at all," Capito insisted. "This is supposed to be a safe, respectable establishment."

The innkeeper tried to intervene with "Sir—"

"If you can't look after people's property," Capito told him, "it's your responsibility to warn them."

"Sir, as I've already explained—"

"You can't expect young ladies to be able to read notices!"

"Please move aside, sir. I need to talk to the young ladies."

Capito said, "You need to shut the gates and have everyone searched."

"The gates are shut, sir. My staff—"

"Your staff are the problem, man! Who else could sneak into a locked room while the guests are at dinner?"

"That's a very serious allegation. I'm going to have to insist that you—"

"It's not an allegation, it's a fact. A valuable necklace—"

"All we have left of our mother's jewellery!" put in Laelia.

"—a family heirloom, has been stolen from one of your rooms while its owner was at dinner."

The innkeeper gestured to his doormen. Neither was as big as Capito but, standing one either side of him, both looked a lot meaner.

The officer stood his ground. "I insist on being present while you talk to these young ladies."

Something about the puffed-out chest reminded Ruso of an outraged pigeon.

"In my office," growled the innkeeper, leading the way.

Stumbling after him, Laelia sobbed, "I wish we'd never come here! I wish we'd stayed at home!"

"It will be all right," her sister assured her. "Our friend is a very important man. He will make them give it back."

"And if they don't," put in Capito, "I would advise your brother to prosecute." He placed a hand on Annia's arm and murmured, "You must tell her not to worry, my dear. I shall see to it that things are put right. One way or another."

It was clear that nobody here was going to need a doctor unless Capito insisted on making trouble, and even then Ruso felt he might let nature take its course. He slipped away and went back to bed, only to be disrupted again when the innkeeper came round to inform them that all the rooms were being searched immediately for a valuable item that had been mislaid.

"Well it's not mislaid in here," pointed out a voice from another bunk.

"Somebody should have taken better care of it," observed another man. "Can't they read?"

"No sir," the innkeeper told him, "they can't. The guests who own it are very upset and we're all doing our best to help."

Ruso sighed and rolled out of bed again.

Finally settling back on his newly-shaken mattress after a fruitless search of the room, he found himself unable to sleep. Relaxing all his muscles in turn didn't work. Deep breathing didn't work. Nothing could distract him from the fact that he was going to have to get up, find a lamp—hopefully there was one burning in the corridor for this very purpose—and make his way back to the latrine.

Ruso woke later than he intended. A subdued group of travellers had already congregated by the time he arrived in the entrance hall, out of breath and with his boots still dangling from one hand. The two women were standing by their luggage. Laelia was puffy-eyed, and Annia's delicate mouth was set in a grim line. Even Capito was silent. Someone's "Did you find it?" was a question framed more out of sympathy than curiosity: it was obvious even before Annia answered that there had been no good news in the night.

"But everyone has been very kind," added Laelia, glancing at Capito. "Especially the good officer here. And the innkeeper did not charge us for the stay."

"I should think not!" muttered another of the other guests.

Ruso had intended to find the innkeeper, but there was no time now. When he got to the latrine, one of last night's room-mates glanced up from his contemplations on the communal seat and gestured toward his bare feet and the boots still in his hand. "In a hurry?"

"Something I ate," Ruso told him, striding toward the corner seat.

The man gave a grunt of sympathy and heaved himself to his feet. "I tell you mate, I'm in no rush to stay here again."

As soon as he was gone Ruso jumped up, stood on the seat and stretched up to grope among the rafters.

Moments later, with his boots hastily and badly tied, he was picking his way through the rubbish that had been dumped in the narrow gap between the latrine building and the outer wall of the yard. The window was higher than he expected. With no time to fetch anything more suitable, he was obliged to trust his weight to an old wooden crate dragged out of a nettle-patch.

Standing on the crate, he was at the perfect height to put one eye to the knot-hole in the shutters. He was rewarded with a clear view of empty seats stretching away into the gloom of the latrine building.

It was a pity he hadn't had time to warn anyone, but now he was here, all he needed to do was wait.

"What you doing?"

Startled, he almost lost his balance. A small girl was staring up at him from the entrance to the gap. "Looking for something," he told her, wondering how long it would be before she fetched an adult, who would have all sorts of ideas about what he was looking for.

"Can I help?"

"You're not tall enough." When she showed no sign of going away, he said, "What are *you* doing?"

She held out a collection of broken sherds of pot. "Hiding the bits before Cook finds out."

"I won't tell," he promised, and resumed his vigil through the knot-hole.

When he turned again she was gone. Too late, he realized that he should have asked her to fetch the innkeeper. It would be embarrassing for any man to be caught in this situation, but for a man with a professional reputation to consider, it would be disastrous. The thought of serving amongst five thousand legionaries who all knew him as the medic caught snooping through latrine windows made him shudder.

The crate gave an ominous crack beneath him. Ruso prayed it would hold long enough for him to witness what was about to happen. Then he prayed that what he was expecting really would happen, because if it didn't, he would have some very awkward explaining to do.

To his relief, the door of the latrine swung open. The muscular slave paused to glance out, then pushed it closed behind him and hurried toward the seat in the corner. Instead of sitting, he too stood on it.

By the time Ruso had made it to the front of the building, the slave was strolling back toward the baggage cart where his mistresses' luggage was waiting to be loaded. The man bent to pick up one of the bags, but exactly what he did as he passed it from one hand to the other in a strangely slow and complicated manner was concealed by his own body. Ruso swore under his breath. Even now, he could not be certain what the man was up to. And still there was no-one around whose help he could recruit.

Across the yard, Capito appeared with a young woman on each arm and they all made their way across to the waiting carriage. Ruso moved forward to intercept them, offering belated sympathy for the loss of the necklace.

"If you could describe it to me," he said, "I'll ask around while I'm travelling. See if anyone knows anything."

Capito looked slightly put out, but the women thanked him for his kind offer. "It's a gold chain," explained Laelia.

"With emeralds set all round it," put in Annia, looking glum. "Our father gave it to our mother after they were married."

"It was the last thing we had," continued her sister. "We had to sell the earrings."

Capito was busy studying the cobblestones. His neck was very pink.

"Oh, I am so sorry! Please don't be upset! It was not your fault in any way!"

Just as Laelia was telling Capito again how kind he had been, a small voice behind Ruso announced, "That's him!"

Any doubt about who 'him' might be was resolved by, "He was spying!"

Before he could move, Ruso felt a hand on his arm. The innkeeper's voice murmured in his ear, "A word, sir?"

One of the doormen had stepped up to block any possible escape.

"I can explain!" Ruso told them as they led him away.

The driver who had just loaded all the baggage onto the cart was less than impressed when the innkeeper ordered the gate to be locked and asked him to unload it all again. Amid much muttering, he spread the bags and boxes in a semicircle on the yard, and then rearranged them into piles as each passenger stepped forward and identified their property.

Finally, under the scrutiny of several impatient drivers, an ostler who was waiting to get two more vehicles under way, a crowd of delayed passengers and an innkeeper who didn't seem inclined to believe him, Ruso stepped forward. Hoping he was right about this, he indicated the bag he had seen the slave pick up after leaving the latrine.

"It can't be that one," said Capito. "That's the young ladies' own bag."

Nobody answered. The young ladies themselves stood in an apparently baffled silence as the innkeeper unfastened the bag. The small girl reappeared from somewhere with a grey blanket, which she spread over the cobbles. The innkeeper crouched, upended the bag and tipped the contents across the blanket.

Everyone peered at the jumble of clothing and sandals and make-up pots and hairpins and little brushes and combs and all the other paraphernalia that women seemed to deem necessary for a long journey. It reminded Ruso of Claudia. There was nothing the least bit remarkable in there.

It was an embarrassing way to begin his career in Britannia. He was aware of people turning to look at him. Waiting for an explanation.

His hopes rose as the innkeeper reached for a fancy sandal with patterns cut into the leather. They sank again as the sandal fell back onto the blanket. He felt heat creeping up his face.

The man picked out the sandal's twin. He squinted inside. Then he upended the sandal over his open palm.

A gold-and-green chain trickled out.

The women rushed forward. "There it is!" cried Laelia. "It's mother's necklace!"

"It's a miracle!" cried her sister. "Oh, thank you, thank you!"

"Amazing," observed the innkeeper, not sounding at all amazed.

"The thief must have put it back!" said Laelia. "Oh, what a relief!" Then, to Ruso, "How did you know?"

Ruso shrugged. "Like your sister said. It's a miracle." He looked her in the eye. "So you won't be needing compensation from your generous friend now, will you?"

"You should have told me last night," observed the innkeeper, lifting the jug to offer a refill of best wine Ruso had tasted since landing in Britannia. Not that it was exceptionally good wine, but some of the rest had been remarkably awful. "My missus was awake half the night worrying about being sued."

"I didn't think of it till everyone had gone to bed," Ruso admitted. "Then I started to wonder why the sisters were comforting each other in Latin when it wasn't their natural tongue."

"Because they were looking for sympathy?"

"They were looking to embarrass Capito," Ruso agreed. "Poor man. I couldn't believe how much money he'd given them."

"Pompous arse."

Ruso shook his head. Capito, it turned out, had only been in Britannia a few days longer than he had himself. Now that the man had been humbled, Ruso's resentment had faded. "He's young, he's new, and he's desperate to impress."

"Then he needs to learn who his friends are. We get a lot of that sort through here. Straight out from Rome, chucking their weight about, demanding services they're not entitled to.

Complaining when the staff don't lick their boots and their backsides." The innkeeper paused to redirect the small girl, who was passing with a pile of laundry. "Here—you don't know who's been telling people my food made him ill, do you?"

"Nobody's said anything to me," said Ruso, truthfully. Then, remembering something else, "If the slave hadn't been making such a fuss in the latrine I wouldn't even have noticed him. But after I heard about the theft I began to wonder whether he really was ill, or whether he was just trying to put me off and get the place to himself. So I got up and went to see where he'd been sitting, and there it was. Tucked away in the rafters."

"We don't get a lot of swindlers," the innkeeper observed. "And those two were bright. First it's all the slave's fault, and then he was only doing it to keep the thing safe and he didn't understand the Latin when matey was blaming himself and offering to pay for a new one."

"I wonder if there really is a brother?" Ruso took a sip of the wine and swilled it around on his tongue. "Maybe the slave *is* the brother."

"They won't get away with it again. Every driver who comes through here'll pass on their description."

Ruso drained the last of his wine and got to his feet. "I'd better get on the road."

The black mare was well turned out and had a lively gait and an intelligent look in her eye, which cheered Ruso considerably until it struck him that he could have said the same of Claudia.

"She's a good horse, boss," the ostler assured him. "You look after her, and she'll look after you."

"Thank you." Ruso glanced up at a scatter of cloud being hurried along by a fresh autumn breeze.

"Nice day for a ride."

"It is." No sea, no females to annoy—Claudia was right: he had certainly annoyed Annia and Laelia—and nobody wanting to show him their ailments.

The man placed a hand on the mare's bridle. "Just one thing before you go, boss. That bag up there." He pointed to the luggage Ruso had strapped to the saddle. "You're not a doctor, are you?"

Ruso hesitated.

"Only I've been having a lot of trouble with this knee…"

Interview with Ruth Downie

Can you tell us a bit about yourself? How long have you been writing and what other jobs have you had?
I started writing when my children were small and one of them now has small children of his own, so that's quite a long time. As for jobs - I trained as a secretary in the days when people actually had secretaries, which seems almost as long ago as Ancient Rome. Still, the touch-typing has come in very handy. Over the years I've done admin jobs and worked in libraries, although the most useful experience from a writing point of view was probably temping in a prison. It was a great insight into working in a large hierarchical organisation with a focus on security. Like, er, the Roman army...

What is it about Rome that inspires you?
The odd contrast between familiarity (town councils and traffic jams and people fiddling their expenses) and strangeness. How can anyone think it's fine to own another human being, or to enjoy seeing people being killed as part of a state-sponsored entertainment? There's also the desire to puncture the arrogance of Romans who felt they had the right to trample over other people's territory - whilst respecting the fact that they did, in their own way, bring all sorts of good things with them.

What inspired you to write this particular story?
I used to be part of a voluntary archaeology group based near the old Roman road that runs north through the midlands (it's now the A5). So over the years I've seen and handled a lot of bits and bobs left behind by the Roman-era travellers. Those people seem very real to me, but I've never managed to think of a story involving them that would fill a whole novel, short stories are different, though. I sent my main character along this road in my first book back in 2006, and being asked to contribute a story to *Rubicon* offered the perfect chance to find out what might have happened to him on the journey.

Can you tell us about your other work inspired by Rome?
I write a series of crime novels about a Roman army medic called Ruso, and his British partner, Tilla. They're based mostly in Roman Britain, although occasionally I've indulged the urge for a longer research trip. To everyone's surprise the first book had a brief flirtation with the New York Times bestsellers list, and there are now eight novels and one novella in the series. I was also part of a team that put together a novel about Boudica, and Simon Turney and I wrote a story together about the Severan campaign in Scotland.

What do you enjoy most about writing?
They say the way to avoid writing cliché is to do plenty of research, but I'd do it anyway because I love it. To be honest my first book started out as three chapters for a "start a novel" competition, but when an agent asked to see the whole thing, I realised I couldn't bluff any longer: I actually needed to know what a doctor in the ancient world would do. That opened up a whole realm of education, fascination and horror. (Cockroach insides to treat earache, anyone?)

If you were transported back to the time your story is set, who is the first person you would want to talk to and why?
Regina, a Catuvellauni tribeswoman from the English midlands. She was first the slave and then the wife of a Syrian trader called Barates. After she died in South Shields at the age of 30, Barates put up a very expensive gravestone to commemorate her. She must have had a fascinating and very varied life and she would know a lot that the Roman historians don't tell us about how the occupiers and the locals found ways of living together.

What would you bring back from ancient Rome with you?
A heightened appreciation of life in the 21st century.

If there was one event in the period you could witness (in perfect safety) what would it be?

When Hadrian toured Britannia in the year 122, several of his top men were sent home in disgrace. We know this had something to do with his wife, but the reasons aren't entirely clear. I'd love to have been there when Hadrian told them why they were being fired.

What are you writing at the moment?

A ninth book in the *Medicus* series.

How important is it for you to be part of a community of writers, and why?

It's essential. Writers are curiously peripheral to the publishing world, so most of our working life is spent on our own with only Facebook and imaginary people for company. Getting together provides encouragement, reassurance and a chance to catch up with the office gossip.

Where can readers find out more about your books?

www.ruthdownie.com

A Brief Affair - Richard Foreman

1.

Rome. 25BC.

Morning.

Sunlight poured through the window of his bedroom, gifting an attractive sheen to the woman's already burnished flesh. Rufus Varro woke, stretched and gulped down a large cup of water, dehydrated from last night's wine.

He heard, in the distance, a couple of carters arguing about their right of way into the street. Neither wanted to give way. The merchants were soon trading insults.

"Cocksucker!"

"Eunuch!"

It was unlikely that the two men would ever be close, if the names they were calling each other were anything to go by, Varro mused. In the distance he could see smoke belching out of the tanneries and bakeries, casting a pall over parts of the city. The nobleman imagined how the populace would be stirring and scurrying along the capital's narrow streets like insects, going about their business. Slaves would be attending to endless onerous duties. Wine vendors and costermongers would be setting out their stalls in the marketplaces. Bleary-eyed drunks would be staggering in or out of taverns. Brothel owners would be kicking out any customers, who had paid to stay overnight. Senators would be rehearsing their speeches, like actors, in front of the mirror, enamoured with the sound of their own voice. They needed to make sure that their policies - and insults towards rivals - were as polished as the marble statues of Augustus which populated Rome.

The alluring woman lying next to him, Sabina, stirred too. Varro considered how the wife of the tax collector, Valerius Glabrio, seemed comfortable and accustomed with waking up in a different bed to her own. The same claim could be made for the priapic aristocrat and poet himself. Even if Varro wasn't so hungover, he would have had trouble remembering the number of lovers he had woken next to over the years (during his time being married, or otherwise).

"Satisfied?" she whispered - or purred - lasciviously, rubbing her shin against his.

Varro breathed in her aromatic perfume, smiled at his new mistress, clasped her hand and kissed her fingertips. As he leaned over to pour out a cup of water for the woman, with his back towards his lover, he yawned.

"Satisfied doesn't come close," the handsome nobleman replied, donning an enamoured expression again.

"Will you compose a poem for me? I want you to immortalise me."

"I'd love to. As long as you do not consider me unfaithful for spending time with my muse instead of you," Varro said, suppressing his instinct to roll his eyes and cringe at his response. He briefly thought about which of his previous poems he could adapt, with minimal effort, to dedicate to the woman. The aristocrat had been part of a generation of poets that considered itself the heir to Catullus. Certainly, Varro drunk as much as his idol. He would spend his evenings at dinner parties hosted by his distinguished neighbours on the Palatine Hill - or the poet would descend into the Suburra to drink, gamble and whore the night away. It had been some time since the "new Catullus" had composed anything of note. Rufus Varro was no longer a poet. Rather, Rufus Varro was a spy.

2.

A day before spending the night with Sabina, Marcus Agrippa summoned the agent to his house. The palatial property had once belonged to Pompey the Great and then Mark Antony. To the victor, the spoils.

Varro was shown to the consul's private chambers. Whilst the recently named Augustus led the armies of Rome on the Spanish frontier, Agrippa had been charged with governing Rome. Caesar's lieutenant had helped win the war, on land and sea, against Mark Antony. Now he was helping to win the peace. As well as managing the grain supply, commissioning various building projects (including new aqueducts, temples and public gardens) and attending to administrative duties to help run the empire - Agrippa also oversaw a network of spies. Sometimes wars are fought in the shadows.

Less than a year ago Varro assisted Agrippa in uncovering a coup against Caesar. He became, in the spymaster's words, "an asset". The reluctant agent had been recruited for other assignments since. Espionage was an essential weapon in the war against the enemies of Rome. It was also a tool to help the aristocrat fight against the enemy of boredom. Augustus himself had recruited his services for certain assignments. The demi-god was not someone to say no to, Varro sagely decided.

Oil lamps hung from the ceiling. Maps of the empire adorned the walls. Marcus Agrippa sat at his desk, which it appeared might soon collapse from the weight of all the parchment, scrolls and wax tablets strewn across it. The consul buried himself in his work, feeling that he owed a duty to both Rome and his close friend. Although Varro believed that work was also a means for Agrippa to escape his grief, from the death of his wife, Caecilia. He had since, at the request of Augustus, married Caesar's niece, Marcella. The decision to take another wife had been borne out of duty to his friend, rather than from any love for the young woman.

A flicker of a smile animated Agrippa's stony expression, as Varro stood before the second most powerful man in the world. Caesar's lieutenant had a reassuring air of resilience and honour about him, like a war horse. He was as straight and efficient as a Roman road, as sturdily built as a Roman column. When he said he was going to do something, he did it - which was rare for a politician, in any age. Agrippa still preferred the company of soldiers to senators and often yearned to be back combating enemies on the battlefield, rather than dealing with the nest of vipers in the Senate House.

"I have an assignment for you, Rufus," Agrippa remarked, without preamble.

Varro sighed to himself, but not with relief.

"I will do my utmost to conceal my excitement," Varro said sarcastically, thinking, however, that sarcasm was the lowest form of sarcasm.

"There is no reason why you should know the name Valerius Glabrio. Glabrio oversees the collection of taxes for the area in and around Patavium. I recently received a couple of complaints about the administrator, accusing him of embezzlement and extortion. However, these testimonies are filled with rumour rather than evidence. Tax collectors are not known for collecting friends. The two merchants who have written to me may bear a personal grievance against Glabrio. Merchants are not known for their honesty and integrity. Should the case come to trial, any half-decent advocate would be able to discredit the witnesses. I do not wish to undermine the authority of our tax system and its administrators by bringing false allegations against Glabrio. But I cannot discount these allegations either.

"I want you to get close to Glabrio's wife, Sabina. Find out what she knows. We need to create a picture of his income and spending, in both Rome and Patavium. I am reliably informed that Sabina is a great beauty - and far from chaste. I'm confident that you will be able to extract the necessary intelligence from her. She will be attending a party, hosted by Lucius Tedius, tomorrow evening. Tedius tells me that Valerius will be absent, attending to his latest mistress. I am sure you're capable of seducing her, or letting her seduce you," Agrippa remarked, whilst glancing at the latest plans to refurbish a temple on the Quirinal Hill. Multi-tasking.

"You may be overestimating my charms."

"And you may be underestimating them. I'm confident that you'll get the job done, one way or another, Rufus. The assignment shouldn't take too long. It will be a brief affair, so to speak... But tell me, how's Manius?" Agrippa said, asking after Varro's bodyguard. The former gladiator, from Britannia, was usually at his friend's side.

"He's happily married, if there is such a state of being. As a belated wedding present, I arranged for Manius and Camilla to spend some time at my villa in Arretium."

"I can assure you that there is such a state of being, albeit it may seem like a brief affair too," Agrippa remarked, picturing his first wife, as opposed to second. "But it's as rare as a courageous Gaul, garrulous Spartan, honest politician or cheerful German. The German sense of humour is no laughing matter."

3.

The wine and conversation flowed at the party, hosted by the senator Lucius Tedius. Patricians and their wives, or mistresses, were out in force. The room was a kaleidoscope of colour and rustling, Chinese silk. Sapphires and amethysts, adorning alabaster necks, sparkled like stars. Serving girls re-filled wine cups and brought around silver trays laden with the latest, fashionable delicacies: octopi in mushroom sauce, spiced cubes of ostrich meat, sea bass infused with saffron and stewed apricots. Melodious harps played in the background. Outside, in the garden, a fire-eater and juggler made spectacles of themselves. Tedius had spared no expense, although, thankfully, their host had failed to arrange a mime to entertain his guests, Varro mused.

The aristocrat saw an old friend, Gaius Macro, and asked him to pick out Sabina.

"Are you on the hunt tonight then?" the former poet, now property developer and inveterate gossip, asked.

"A man needs his sport," Varro replied, burdened by his reputation, as opposed to proud of it.

"A married man needs his sport too. Unfortunately, my wife has ruined my evening again by insisting on coming along tonight. Instead of being hurled from the Tarpeian Rock, Rome should just compel its enemies to marry, as a punishment. You were right to divorce and regain your freedom."

Varro forced a smile, whilst experiencing his own sense of grief as he thought about his former wife, Lucilla. He had lost the only woman he had ever loved. Ever would love. Yet Lucilla was right to divorce him, to be free of him. Even before Varro became a spy, he was duplicitous.

The agent spotted Sabina across the crowded room and duly pretended to be entranced, enamoured. The wife of Valerius Glabrio was indeed a great beauty. Kohl-black tendrils of hair framed an olive complexion and sculptured features. Her pouting lips were ripe for kissing. Her V-necked gown showed off a diamond pendant, as well as other assets. Sabina stared at the handsome stranger, appreciatively.

"I don't suppose you know anything about her husband?" Varro remarked to Macro.

"I have met him on a couple of occasions, which were two too many. Glabrio is fond of talking about money. He would probably sell his own mother - and put her up for auction to obtain the best price - if he thought he'd profit from the deal. I have known poets to be less arrogant too. By all means cuckold the odious official."

Varro had every intention of doing so.

"It seems that you have already had plenty of hopeful - and hopeless - would-be suitors engage you this evening. I'm not sure which to class myself as, but I was wondering if you would take pity on me, as someone who is attending the party alone, and let me keep you company? My name is Rufus Varro."

The woman smiled, and even seemed a little coy. But not too coy. Varro also noticed a glimmer of recognition in her eyes as he said his name. Sabina had indeed heard of him. One of her friends had slept with the famous (or infamous) nobleman and poet, a year ago. "He was a fun and passionate lover... I hoped to unlock his heart, or his treasury, but we soon grew bored with one another," her friend remarked, tinged with regret.

Sabina eyed the handsome poet up, as if assessing the value of a statue. She had once sat as an artist's model and been sculptured. She fancied how the poet might be able to immortalise her in verse.

"I am Sabina. I have come unaccompanied too. My husband is devoting himself to one of his mistresses this evening," she tartly remarked. What is good enough for the goose is good enough for the gander, Sabina judged.

Varro continued to talk to the woman. Agrippa was right to state that she was a great beauty, although he failed to mention how she was no great wit. Despite her statuesque figure most of his jokes still went over her head. He feigned interest in her life, whilst wheedling information out of her. The reluctant agent was also an accomplished one. She mentioned how her husband had bought the tellingly expensive diamond pendant around her neck, that it had originally been a gift from Caesar to Servilia. The elaborate gold earrings hanging from her ears had once belonged to Cleopatra. Glabrio may not have showered his wife with too much time and attention, but he did shower her with gifts. Varro was all too aware of the exorbitant expense of maintaining both a wife and mistress.

Whether the desire-fuelled look in her eyes was borne from the wine, or lust, the agent didn't much care. The hunter had snared his prey. The party began to thin out. Sabina accepted Varro's invitation to come back to his villa. It was a short trip to travel across the Palatine Hill. A few of the litter bearers smirked, as they heard the noises the woman emitted behind the curtains. But they had heard it all before. Sabina also gasped on witnessing the size of the aristocrat's house. More than one mistress, over the years, had swooned upon realising how wealthy the poet was.

4.

Sabina beamed with delight, and then kissed the poet in gratitude, at the news that he would compose a poem especially for her. Hopefully her friends would be bitterly jealous. When she planted a second kiss on his lips, she slid her hand beneath the bedsheet. The woman was insatiable, Varro thought to himself. But there were worse traits a lover could own. One was having an irate husband, trying to bash down your door.

Fronto, Varro's wizened estate manager, calmly knocked on his master's door and conveyed that the lady's husband was currently at the front of the house, along with a couple of his attendants. Fronto had seen it all before. Usually Manius had been present, however, in such circumstances. The bodyguard had been proficient over the years in dealing with any unwelcome callers.

Varro gazed at Sabina with genuine concern, her aspect now filled with fear rather than lust. Her burnished flesh somehow seemed paler. A wave of dread crashed against Varro's heart too as he remembered Cassandra. The fate of his former mistress still haunted him. Her husband had tortured and murdered his wife, after she helped to uncover his plot to overthrow Caesar.

All was not lost, however. Varro instructed Fronto to hide Sabina in the wine cellar. As much as his slaves might be tempted to do so, they were not to confront Glabrio's bodyguards. Varro would lead their unwelcome guests away from the house.

Varro's heart was beating, but not with ardour, as he dressed and climbed out the window. He soon heard Glabrio cursing his name at the gates to his house. He called the aristocrat any number of names - bastard, coward, degenerate. Varro fleetingly thought how it would be difficult for him to find an advocate who could successfully argue against any of the tax collector's assertions.

Glabrio stood at the tall, iron gates to the property. The official screwed-up countenance was flushed, either from anger or the wine from the night before. He barked and growled, threatening violence on a whey-faced slave if he didn't let him in. Glabrio was close to ordering his bodyguards to rip the gate off its hinges or clamber over it.

The wronged - and wronging - husband still clasped the note he had received that morning, after coming home from spending the evening with his mistress. The sender stated he wished to remain anonymous - but he owed a duty to Glabrio to write to him. The letter informed that his wife had left the party last night with the aristocrat Rufus Varro. The sender had also overheard Varro malign Glabrio throughout the evening, how he couldn't afford to keep his wife in the lifestyle she deserved. He was just "a provincial bureaucrat." The nobleman made a boast of turning the official into a cuckold - and writing about the affair in a poem.

Glabrio's blood was quickly brought to the boil and he ordered his bodyguards to accompany him, as he marched through the streets of Rome in order to confront the ignoble aristocrat and collect his whorish wife. The tax collector would not have his dignity and authority impugned. He riled, as he imagined the laughter, from friends and enemies alike, should they read a satirical verse about the affair. Glabrio would deal with his wife accordingly. But first he would deal with the arrogant, upstart poet. He would have his attendants beat him - and he himself would thrash Varro, like he was an errant child, for his transgressions. The tax collector would of course wait until his bodyguards could hold his victim down, before metering out the punishment.

Glabrio witnessed a figure climbing over the garden wall and rightly suspected it was Varro. As he reached the top of the wall he glanced back at the gate. The bodyguards were ex-soldiers or ex-gladiators. Their tunics were stretched across their muscular bodies. Violence was a way of life. They were probably kept busy, guarding the unpopular tax collector or bullying and extorting money out of people.

Varro and Glabrio locked eyes. The latter's snarl turned into a wolfish grin. There would be no escape for the dissolute poet. Glabrio smelled blood. The hunt was on.

5.

Sweat dripped from his brow, his lungs and thighs began to burn, as Varro raced through the streets of the Palatine. He frequently looked back to chart the progress of his two pursuers. Although the bodyguards were large, they were far from lumbering. They were slowly and surely gaining ground, like an incoming tide about to drown him. He even began to hear the sound of their sandals slap against the paving stones.

At least the first part of his plan had succeeded. He had drawn the assailants away from the house. Fronto, Sabina and his slaves were safe. He just needed to get through the day with his bones intact. Varro cut through a few narrow alleys and descended into the bowels of the Subura. He was starting to tire. His legs nearly gave way, twice, as he ran along a cobblestoned street. Varro darted around a corner, into a high-walled courtyard. As he turned back towards the entrance, he was confronted by the two bodyguards, Hanno and Pollux, forming a human barrier to trap him on all sides. They panted, like hounds, and drew their cudgels. Varro was without his dagger.

Perhaps he was too exhausted, or frightened, to take on the brutal looking Hanno, whilst his confederate retraced his steps and fetched his master. Varro waited, his head bowed down like a condemned man awaiting a guilty verdict. A gust of wind kicked up some dust in the courtyard. The temperature dropped, but that wasn't necessarily the reason why a chill ran down his spine.

Glabrio's ire was replaced by an air of triumph when he witnessed how forlorn the aristocrat appeared. He imagined that the satirical poet had mocked him, in front of his wife, last night. But who was laughing now?

"I hope this will teach you a lesson. There is nothing that a man can take, that a tax collector cannot take back. Including his wife. I have encountered your kind before. You noblemen think you are entitled to everything or everyone."

The official was relishing his ability to sneer at and punish someone from the privileged classes, who had once haughtily looked down their noses at him.

"Sabina doesn't love you," Varro exclaimed.

Glabrio laughed, before replying.

"Ha! This shows how much poets know about love. Sabina's my wife, she's not supposed to love me. She is only supposed to obey me, which she has failed to do - and will pay the price. Everything has a price."

"If everything has a price, will you allow me to buy my way out of this? Can we not negotiate a settlement, for me to purchase my freedom? I would also be willing to pay you, so I can still see your wife. I am a man of considerable wealth. I can ensure Sabina is kept in a style deserving of her beauty. Surely, as a tax collector, you do not possess the means to give her everything that she wants?"

Glabrio laughed again, even louder.

"You might be surprised by how much I earn. And I have earned my wealth, instead of merely inheriting it, like you. At my villa in Patavium I have a personal treasury, which would rival yours. Corruption is rife across the empire, as plentiful as the air we breathe. We bid for the opportunity to collect taxes. It is only natural and just that we should pay ourselves a bonus for our work and investment. I have more money that I know what to do with. Because I have other people's money."

"Is that enough?" Varro asked.

"What do you mean, is that enough? Man is man. We always want more. And I will take more," Glabrio argued, creasing his face in either contempt or confoundment.

"He wasn't talking to you," Marcus Agrippa remarked, appearing from over the wall. "That will indeed be enough, Rufus. Thank you."

A couple of archers flanked the consul, training their bows on the dumbstruck bodyguards. Their barrel chests were no longer puffed out in confidence. A group of praetorians blocked the entrance to the courtyard, forming a human barrier. Ire replaced the tax official's air of triumph. The smile fell from his face, as swiftly as an executioner's sword plunging down onto a neck.

Varro breathed a sigh of relief. His plan had worked. The agent had been the author behind the anonymous letter to Glabrio. As they had pre-arranged, Fronto had sent a slave to deliver the message, once the estate manager had seen Sabina accompany his master back to the house. Varro, who was all too familiar with the neighbourhood of the Suburra, had deliberately led the bodyguards into the courtyard. To seemingly trap himself. Given the arrogant, boastful nature of the official - he was more conceited than a poet - Varro hadn't found it too difficult to prise a confession from his target. The fish had taken the bait.

As if Glabrio's testimony wouldn't damn him enough, Agrippa would soon give the order for his house in Patavium to be searched. The official's wealth would be appropriated by the state. It was unlikely that the extorted and embezzled monies would be returned to the bureaucrat's victims. Render unto

Caesar what's Caesar's. Agrippa would ensure that Glabrio would not punish his wife for his own transgressions. He would also warn the tax collector against being tempted to exact any revenge on Varro. The agent had enough enemies to contend with already.

The affair - the brief affair - was over.

Interview with Richard Foreman

Can you tell us a bit about yourself? How long have you been writing and what other jobs have you had?

Although I wrote my first book in my early twenties, I have been writing professionally for the past seven years or so. Most of the jobs I've had have been related to the book trade. I've worked as a bookseller, publicist, literary consultant and publisher. Suffice to say I've attended a lot of dinners and launch parties. If only my sales were as high as my cholesterol levels.

What is it about Rome that inspires you?

Rome resonates, in relation to its power politics, empire building, and bread and circuses, among other things. Romans could be urbane, bawdy, cultured, witty and sarcastic – like Londoners. Similar to the other authors included in this collection, Romans also had a love of history and storytelling. The city was a melting pot, which sometimes boiled over. One also can't help but be inspired by some of the figures populating Rome's history. Julius Caesar, Cicero and Augustus could be vain-glorious and ruthless – but they were seldom dull.

Can you tell us about your other work inspired by Rome?

I've written several series set during Ancient Rome now. The Augustus books. The Sword of Rome series, based around the campaigns of Julius Caesar. And Sword of Empire, which covers the life of Marcus Aurelius and has been described as an unofficial prequel to Gladiator. As well as covering the lives of the Emperors, the books also focus on soldiers and military history. The current series, Spies of Rome, are a slight departure in that the books double-up as crime stories.

What do you enjoy most about writing?

It stops me from getting a proper job. I enjoy most aspects of writing: the research, creating stories/characters and receiving feedback from readers. The writing community is largely a fun and generous one too.

If you were transported back to the time your story is set, who is the first person you would want to talk to and why?

Marcus Agrippa. I would like to thank him for helping me generate so many book sales over the years. Also, even more than Augustus, Agrippa helped turn Rome from a city of stone into one of marble. He was accomplished as a soldier, shipbuilder, architect and statesman. Most people can't even get the latter right, especially in this day and age.

What would you bring back from ancient Rome with you?

Hopefully not the pox. I've always been curious as to what a Trojan Pig would taste like. The book buyer - and book seller - in me would also want to pick up a few first editions by Cicero.

If there was one event in the period you could witness (in perfect safety) what would it be?

Due to my cowardice, both moral and physical, I would probably avoid any battles. The obvious answer would be the Ides of March. There are various other events which I have written about, such as Cicero delivering his Philippics and the death of Marcus Aurelius, which would've been interesting - and useful - to experience too.

What are you writing at the moment?

I am currently writing the third and final book in the Spies of Rome trilogy. It's fun to bring various characters and strands of plot together. Rufus Varro has evolved throughout the books, although some of the jokes are the same. I have also started to read and research things for my next series, which will be set during the First Crusade. Having written about Henry V and Agincourt, I'm looking forward to returning to the medieval period – and writing the same old jokes.

How important is it for you to be part of a community of writers, and why?

I have been remarkably fortunate over the years to have known a number of writers who I admire, on a personal and professional level. Going back to my days as a bookseller, I was one of the first people to champion Conn Iggulden and his Emperor series. As a publicist I promoted several authors writing about Ancient Rome, including Tom Holland and Simon Scarrow. In meeting the likes of Bernard Cornwell and Steven Saylor you not only pick up on things relating to the craft of writing, but they also provide you with a guide in how to behave as an author – with professionalism and decency. For any would-be writers out there, it is not only important to be part of a community of writers - but it's fun.

Where can readers find out more about your books?

My books are available on Amazon of course. Readers can get in touch via twitter too, @rforemanauthor Like most authors I'm happy to hear from readers. Not least please let me know what you think about A Brief Affair and other stories in this collection.

Mystery of Victory - Alison Morton

Rome, AD395

'No!'

A tall man about forty years, Lucius Apulius, a young senator from an old family, darted forwards to block the soldiers. The centurion drew his sword and thrust it in Apulius's face. The tip travelled down to touch the skin at the base of Apulius's throat. The young senator didn't flinch, but an arm as inflexible as iron barred him going further. His father.

'Sheath your sword, centurion,' Apulius senior commanded. 'The Curia is no place for weapons.'

The soldier snorted. 'Begging your honour's pardon,' he said, 'but that don't mean much these days. I take my orders from the Augustus. Stand aside.'

Neither of the Apulii moved. The centurion sheathed his sword and moved away to supervise the legionaries shuffling round them, sweating as they pulled a builder's handcart up the steps and between the banks of seating towards the altar of Victory.

The statue soared over them, golden, wings outstretched, one leg forward, escaping her wind-caught robe, her feet barely touching the globe. Victory's arm, bent at a shallow angle at the elbow, offered the laurel crown to the winner. In her other hand, she grasped a palm branch, the tip resting on her shoulder.

When the Romans seized her after Pyrrhus of Epirus abandoned her in Tarentum, she ceased being Nike, who had fought alongside the Olympian gods against the Titans, and became Victory. Octavian brought her to his city after defeating the Egyptian queen Cleopatra and her lover Marcus Antonius. When he recast himself as Augustus, he placed golden Victory in the Senate and recast her as the symbol of Rome, her *numen*. While she stood, Rome would never fall.

Fresh from his victory at the Frigidus River, four hundred years after his god was born, Theodosius the Christian had marched into the Senate, paused and stared at the statue of Victory with his hard fanatic's eyes.

Now, twenty of Theodosius' soldiers plodded into the Curia. They ignored the shocked faces of the senators whose first loud protests faded to mutterings, which died when the centurion gave a curt command to the work party to line the approach to the ancient square altar, swords out and ready.

'In Jupiter's name, stop!' the younger Apulius shouted, the only one to break the silence.

The centurion turned slowly, a cynical look on his face as he looked Apulius up and down. The only sound in the *curia* came from metal on cloth and the creak of leather boots. Every eye was on the two men.

'Jupiter? That old women's tale?' the centurion said after a pause. He snorted. 'Christ is our God, and the only one. You'd do well to remember that. Sir.' He added in a tone half a breath off a sneer.

He flicked his fingers impatiently at the four legionaries surrounding the altar. They hesitated. A trace of incense hung in the air as it had for hundreds of years. They glanced at the watching senators, the walls, the floor, each other, but none dared to look up at Victory. Apulius wished she would come off her globe and take flight, scattering them like panicking sheep.

When the centurion barked at them to get on with it, two of them grasped the statue's legs and skirts with their nervous hands and lifted it off the square altar. Solid gold, it almost slid from their grasp and thumped to the floor. The youngest legionary glanced down at the statue and drew his right thumb across his forehead in a crossing motion. Apulius glared at him and the boy looked away, a pink tinge on his cheeks.

The two other soldiers hefted the altar into the handcart like a piece of building stone. The first two turned the statue on its face as if Victory was diving to her death. Apulius and his father watched grimly as she was manhandled out through the door on to a second cart. Some senators muttered amongst themselves, staying in tight knots of twos and threes in the centre but others resumed their usual seats, ready to pass to the next item of business. Christians, Apulius thought; they formed the majority after all. But they'd all felt the breath of history as something of its power had passed before them and vanished. He turned quickly away from his father's solemn gaze knowing that he, too, wept in his heart.

Just past midnight, Lucius Apulius and his friend Gaius Mitelus eased open the high gates of the imperial contractor's yard. Down one side ran open-ended bins with sand, small stones and loose materials, then lean-tos with blocks of stone, marble, red curved tiles piled up. Across the entire back of the yard lay the workshop, solid stone and red tile roof bleached silver in the moonlight. Outside, a horse whinnied. Apulius cursed. Mitelus hushed him.

'Pluto, if that watchman or some bastard of a patrol comes this way, we're ash in the sacred flame,' Apulius hissed.

An empty threat – the Vestals' holy flame had been extinguished after a thousand years. Theodosius's men had already expelled Coelia Concordia, the last *Vestalis Maxima* from the holy College of Vestals and sealed the temple door.

'Let's get on, then,' Mitelus retorted, 'instead of waiting like nervous sixteen-year-olds on their first brothel visit.'

Apulius turned the 'borrowed' key in the lock of the workshop door. Both winced as it clicked loudly. The two men crept in, letting the moonlight slip in for a second. Door closed, Mitelus struck a fire steel and lit a taper, a thin, poor thing like a military field torch. The smoky flickering light was enough to throw up shadows of lifting braces, hammers, chisels, saws and axes – and Mitelus's face.

He wove his way through the jumble of half-worked stone, parts of columns, and a chipped statue with one arm. Struggling towards the back, he tripped over one of the large wedges used for splitting stone. He threw his hand out and found a wing. His fingers explored and found the delicate feathering.

'Jupiter!' He steadied himself, coughing with the dust. 'Apulius. I've found her.'

Murmuring a swift prayer to Fortuna, they swaddled the statue in rough sacking and carried it across the yard. The tall gate creaked, then thudded as it closed behind them in the deserted street.

'Where the Hades is this driver of yours?' Gaius Mitelus's voice was strong but anxious. 'Can we trust him?'

'Nobody better,' Apulius answered.

'Everybody's trustworthy until they get paid enough not to be, or it's beaten out of them.'

'I'd put my life in Titus Calavius's hands.'

'You may well have done tonight.'

'For Mars' sake, Gaius, he served with me up on the Danube, then in Noricum. Despite his loyal service, he was passed over several times because he wouldn't fully embrace the Galilean way. Believe me, if he said he'll be here, he'll be here.'

The sound of wheels on the street stopped their bickering. A horse snickered and a dilapidated four-wheel cart approached, its driver's face hidden in a hood.

'*Merda*, I thought you'd been caught,' Apulius said as he climbed up. He sniffed. 'Speaking of shit, where the hell did you get this wagon?'

'Ha! It's the one the stable uses for shovelling dung,' the driver said and flung back the hood to reveal Calavius's grin. 'Good disguise, no? Nobody will want to inspect it.'

Apulius laughed.

'Go!' Mitelus smacked the horse's rump and leapt on the back as the wagon started moving.

The Greek's studio was not far. He sniffed over-delicately when Apulius and Mitelus pulled the sacking away from the statue.

'This is a copy, I presume?' the Greek said. His eyes had widened as he studied the figure, assessing every fold and curve and feeling the feather patterning, the delicate working of the laurel wreath.

Apulius snorted.

'We'd hardly be able to bring you the original, would we?' he said. Mitelus stood silent, his arms crossed. The Greek said nothing but looked from one Roman to another.

'Ten days,' he said at last. 'Double for keeping quiet.'

The Greek worked, tapping and chipping. Small pieces of stone plinked on to the flagstones. A curse erupted now and then. He darted back and forth looking at the statue the Romans had brought him, sometimes making sketches, then back to his chipping and tapping. But now and again, he stood for several minutes just staring at it.

He boiled glue, beat and ground metal. He brushed his new creation's figure with paint, lapping and dabbing. On the late afternoon of the tenth day, the Greek finally laid down his tools, poured himself a cup of wine and flopped down on his couch. The work had been hard, and the evening was sultry. He dozed.

'Not interrupting you, are we?' A voice demanded. The Greek sat up, his head spinning. Apulius and Mitelus loomed over him, dressed like workmen in dull serviceable tunics and frayed leather belts. They walked round the Greek's new creation as he lit a lamp and brought it close so they could see the detail.

'Not bad. Paint's a bit dull, though,' Mitelus said.

'I've made it as near as possible to your original without using gold itself. You can't expect more.'

'Really?' Mitelus said. 'We're paying you enough.'

'Leave it, Gaius.' Apulius said. 'We need to get loaded up.'

After wrapping the new figure in sacking and laying it in the cart, Apulius jumped up beside Calavius. The younger man turned and gave a cheery wave and smile to Mitelus who watched expressionless as the cart disappeared in the dust.

'You want a drink?' the Greek said, interrupting Mitelus's thoughts.

'Yes, then we'll get on.'

Mitelus stood in front of golden Victory, suddenly overcome by the impiety of what he had to do. He gestured to the Greek, who placed a pot and brush in front of the statue and waited. To the artisan's astonishment, Mitelus bowed to the statue.

Forgive us for what we must do. It is only to save you.

He bent down, dipped the brush in the mixture and covered the statue in glutinous grey paint. Before it could dry, he and the Greek showered it with chalk powder and fine grit. Then another coat of paint, then grey sand and lime. They obliterated the gold, the fine feathering, the sheen of her robe. Mitelus didn't say another word. He stayed in the Greek's studio that night, bedded down on a mattress with his sword inches from his hand.

Apulius returned the next day in the afternoon. He nodded in reply to Mitelus's raised eyebrow and questioning look. The two of them checked the surface of the statue was dry and wrapped it in soft cloths, then sacking. Coins clinked as Apulius handed over a heavy purse. He nodded to the Greek. 'Our thanks for your work. The gods reward you.'

'Let's hope they protect me when I'm arrested for forgery,' the Greek muttered under his breath as he watched the two men leave in their cart.

The figure stood for weeks in Apulius's garden, just another dull statue, covered some days in frost, others in rain and growing a thin coat of moss.

A month later, a girl, twelve or thirteen years old, red-gold curls running all over her head and down her back, pelted along the garden path. She stopped in front of the statue. She glanced backward, then jumped into the shrubs behind it and crouched down, leaning against the plinth. A young woman, darker, hurried down the path.

'Julia Apulia,' she called out. 'If you don't come out now from where you're hiding, you're going to get such a whipping my arm will ache.'

The child trembled.

'Galla?' A man's voice. Apulius.

'Father.' She dropped her eyes for a second, but raised them almost immediately. 'It's Julia. She's run off again.'

'Darling, I don't think she's the type to sit indoors on a sunny day, learning her letters or sewing cloth.'

'How can you be so tolerant? She's immodest, unruly—'

'And full of spirit,' he finished, his mouth smiling, but his eyes bleak. Perhaps he remembered his dead wife, the first Julia, the tough daughter of the Celtic princeling Bacausus. She had left her native Noricum, pursued the young Tribune Apulius to Rome and married him. Revelling in her three daughters, she knew her Roman husband had needed a son. But having tried for the fourth time, she went into the shades the night little Julia was born.

Apulius smiled at his serious eldest daughter and took her hand. 'Peace, Galla. We have so little time here.'

When the buds on the roses started to split, two servants came for the statue and wrapped it in blankets, folding rough cloth round the wings, head and the delicate palm leaf. They padded the whole figure with wadding and laid it in a freshly made pinewood box.

They travelled in wagons for several weeks – four hundred men, women and children – leaving Rome and its Christians forever. Rolling first along metalled roads, crossing bridges, they trekked up passes and along ox trails towards the mountains. Horses galloped alongside, goats, cows and fractious children adding to the noise and dust. Little Julia rode in the wagon with the statue, sitting or lying on a pile of blankets and cushions, her hand resting on the box, sometimes telling the statue stories about her past and possible future, about the twelve families travelling together, the squabbling and the sharing on the journey north. People started calling it 'Julia's wagon'. Sometimes she walked alongside, but never ventured far from it; other times the sound of soft, rhythmic breathing intervened when despite the jolting wagon, the child fell asleep. At dusk, when they stopped to camp for the night, one of her sisters would fetch the exhausted child to her pallet in their tent.

One evening, after Apulius had said goodnight to his daughters, he wove in between the tents and wagons on the way to his own tent to hold council with the heads of the other families. He pulled his cloak tighter against the cold wind. They were only in the foothills. He must be getting old, he thought. Next, he'd be considering putting on barbarian breeches to keep warm, the gods forbid! He glanced up at the moon; full, almost bursting. Perhaps that was why the entire train had been bad-tempered, or maybe it was boredom and exhaustion combined. He raised his arm and murmured a prayer to Abeona, goddess of outward journeys. She not only protected travellers but had also watched over each of his daughters as they'd taken their first steps. He added one to Mercury to protect his group during their transition. The god knew they'd need it. Had it been folly to leave Rome and everything they knew?

Just as he turned away, he caught a light across the valley. Strange, they were no farms, or even peasant huts, just grass, and some woods, all turned white by the bright moon. Another glint to its left. No, a reflection. Then he heard a faint clink of metal. Pluto in Tartarus. Weapons. He ran to the nearest sentry Mitelus had posted round the camp.

'Quick, but quiet. Rouse your sector, but no noise or talking. Full weapons. And muster here.'

Apulius didn't wait but pelted towards the centre of the camp. He burst into his tent where his comrades were waiting. Mitelus was pouring a cup of wine and laughing at a joke Calavius had made.

'Stop. We may be under attack.'

'Where?' snapped Mitelus.

'North perimeter, facing the mountains.'

Mitelus nodded at the others. They grasped their weapons, pushed out of the tent and disappeared.

'I hope your defence plan works, Gaius,' Apulius said, frowning.

'My dear Lucius, I have a cup of wine waiting for me. And I fully intend to finish it,' Mitelus said, one eyebrow raised. 'Of course, we will prevail. If not, we will die nobly.' But there was a bitter tone to his voice. 'Now, to your sector and your post.'

Two arms around her waist pulling her middle up into the folds of a blanket. Julia jolted awake in the dark of the night. Half-whispers, half-shouts surrounded her as she was pressed against her oldest sister Galla's body who ran with her. Clashing weapons, a violent swerve as Galla made for the wagon. The young woman thrust the bundled child through the leather flap at the back of her wagon.

'Stay hidden, behind wooden crate,' Galla said in an urgent whisper. 'You must stay as still as Victory until I fetch you.'

'Don't leave me, Galla,' Julia pleaded.

'She will protect you. I must go and fight.'

Clashes of metal on metal, women's and men's shouting. Eventually, the noise faded. Galla returned just before dawn, her face dirty and a smear of blood on her cheek. Julia was fast asleep, her arm across the statue's box and her face peaceful. The child and the goddess had protected each other.

Ten days later, they entered the oppidum at Virunum and set up a temporary camp. Before he rested or even took a drink, Apulius drew back the heavy bolt across the door of a large outbuilding and gestured the driver of Julia's wagon in. Leather creaked as they unfastened the traces and lifted the yokes to release the oxen. They re-bolted the door and Apulius murmured a short prayer as he left.

The next day, two men unpacked the statue and set it on a low pedestal in between two yew trees overlooking a wide river valley. The air was fresher – mixed with wood-smoke, animals, olives and pine resin. Before the statue were mountains, not the scraped dry crusts of Hellas where Victory as Nike had originated, but lush, green meadows full of delicate purple and yellow flowers.

Julia brought a tall grey-haired man to see the statue. Bearded, and wearing a thick gold torc around his neck, he was no Roman. Her soft, almost babyish hand nestled in the big man's paw.

'Grandfather, this is my friend. Everybody calls her Victory, but in her head she's Nike. She keeps us safe.'

They built their town, Roma Nova, crude at first, only a *decumanus maximus,* a main street, crossed by a smaller one but it grew. They bred warrior sons and daughters who defended their valley from would-be invaders. Mitelus died in battle six years after arriving; his friend Apulius, their leader, their imperator, was stricken by wounds. Apulius' daughters, Galla, Lucilla, Claudia and not so little Julia, prayed in front of Victory, their faces strained, their bodies clad in chain shirts and leather breeches, swords at their waists. Like their mother's family and her mother's before her, they went into battle with their male cousins and friends against invading barbarians. They won, but at great cost.

When Julia Apulia was a grandmother of fifty with white and grey hair interwoven with fading red, she came to see the statue in the garden. She limped and leaned heavily on a stick. Clutching her free hand was a girl, about eleven or twelve years old, with Julia's red hair, but darker, brown with copper burnt too long.

Julia bowed to the statue, slowly and stiffly.

'This is my dead son's child, Cloelia Mitela, also the granddaughter of Gaius Mitelus who rescued you all those years ago.' Julia raised her eyes up to the unseeing ones of Victory. 'I hope you will be her friend like you have been mine.' She closed her eyes for a moment. Her face sagged. She looked old, well beyond her natural age, from a hard life and many battles.

She beckoned forward two men and an overgrown adolescent carrying cloths, buckets and builders' tools.

'This is Victory,' Julia said to them, 'our spirit, our guardian. You are to clean her with the utmost care until she shines through.'

The men exchanged glances for several seconds, then laid cloths around the base, picked up their tools and started chipping at the grey crust. The boy climbed on to a stool, raised his small hammer and sculptor's chisel. With his first tap on the concrete coating, he shattered the statue's wing.

Julia blenched and swayed. Cloelia wrapped her arms around her grandmother's waist and cried out, 'Nonna!'

'Get that oaf a hundred miles from me,' Julia hissed.

One workman bundled the boy away. Cloelia bent down and gently picked up the shattered gold and cement feathers. She instructed the other workman to take the statue to the master smith and walked by the cart to his studio, supporting the furious Julia and speaking soft words to her.

When the smith shook his head, Cloelia insisted he attempt the repair. She came every day with Julia, watching gravely as they tried and failed four times. They hadn't rediscovered the gold seams mined and abandoned by their forebears, so they had no gold to use. Reluctantly, but not daring to cross Julia, the smith used precious silver clawed out of the new mine. The fifth attempt was clumsy and painted, but he succeeded. A sorry state of affairs, but the new colony sacrificed its tiny wealth for Victory.

The day before the statue's final journey, Cloelia came alone. 'Nonna can't come today. She's sick and has to stay in bed.' Her shoulders drooped, but she managed to smile up at the statue's face 'I'll come and see you tomorrow when you're in the new Senate House.'

Tall stone walls rose to double height, topped with a red tile roof. Columns at each corner supported the covered public forecourt rising from wide steps at the formal entrance. Dominating the inner hall stood a new square pedestal, polished and gleaming, widening out at the top with a shallow dip carved out for offerings. Two women and two men lifted Victory on to the altar. She soared over the people who had saved her. It was as if she had sworn to protect them to the last ounce of her power, until the end of days.

Imperatrix Galla and her two sisters, Lucilla and Claudia, their daughters and sons, senior members of the Twelve Families who as children had made the long trek from Rome, stood in silence before the altar. The priestess poured a libation, dropped a pinch of incense and intoned ritual prayers.

After the adults left after the ceremony, Cloelia laid myrtle leaves at the foot of the altar.

'Nonna couldn't be here to see you in your proper place.' Her face glistened with tears. 'She crossed the Styx last night, but before she went, she begged Great Aunt Galla not to stop your re-dedication. She said it was her life's dream.'

Cloelia bowed her dark copper head, wiped her hand across her eyes, turned and escaped through the public forecourt. She stumbled down the steps into her mother's arms.

As the sun set, another slight girl, with translucent red-gold curls that didn't reflect the dusk light, came and settled by the altar. She cast no shadow and almost merged into the stone. She looked up and smiled. Victory bent her head towards the girl and smiled down at her.

Interview with Alison Morton

Can you tell us a bit about yourself? How long have you been writing and what other jobs have you had?

A bad film triggered my novel writing career in 2009. The Roma Nova alternative history story had been bubbling away in my head for decades, almost as long as I'd become a 'Roman nut' at age eleven. The idea of a 21st century woman Praetorian driving events in a modern Roman society was, and is, such a tempting idea.

In the middle of selling my translation business in 2009, I turned out (possibly churned out) 90,000 words from a hidden place inside me. Eight books later...

Before that? Soldier, City of London export credits insurer, civil servant, coin and medal dealer, translator, business owner. Somewhere along the way, I gathered a first degree in French, German and Economics and a masters' in history.

What is it about Rome that inspires you?

Longevity, complexity, their love of systems and purpose, their high ideals and high culture, their ceaseless thirst for intrigue, conspiracy and power, their ability to adapt, sacrifice and grasp.

What inspired you to write this particular story?

A bad film, even though Ewan McGregor co-starred, building on being able to 'alternate' history (blame Robert Harris and *Fatherland*) and ingrained feminism, and even further back, that glorious mosaic pavement in Ampurias shining under a hot sun that inspired a lifelong fascination for Ancient Rome.

(https://alison-morton.com/2015/10/11/what-inspired-roma-nova/)

What do you enjoy most about writing?

The new places you go, virtually and physically, the new people you meet and the new things you learn when researching. Otherwise, the satisfaction of getting your story out in a reasonably coherent form. Best of all, letting your imagination soar and immersing your whole mind in a different place and era.

If you were transported back to the time your story is set, who is the first person you would want to talk to and why?

I'd love to talk to Symmachus (Quintus Aurelius Symmachus) about his leading the (sadly unsuccessful) senatorial delegation of protest in AD 391 against Gratian, when the latter ordered the Altar of Victory removed from the *curia* in the Forum Romanum. Plus, if there was time, to learn more about Symmachus's exchange of letters with Ambrosius of Milan two years later when the former made a famous appeal to Gratian's successor, Valentinian II, for tolerance of traditional Roman religion.

If there was one event in the period you could witness (in perfect safety) what would it be?

To have heard Hypatia of Alexandria speak and/or teach would have been an enormous privilege. *"Having succeeded to the school of Plato and Plotinus, she explained the principles of philosophy to her auditors, many of whom came from a distance to receive her instructions. On account of the self-possession and ease of manner which she had acquired in consequence of the cultivation of her mind, she not infrequently appeared in public in the presence of the magistrates. Neither did she feel abashed in going to an assembly of men. For all men on account of her extraordinary dignity and virtue admired her the more."*

(Socrates of Constantinople: Ecclesiastical History)

Why do you think readers are still so thirsty for stories from this period?

Rome fascinates across its 1229 years' existence in the West, hence so many plays, events, research, reconstruction, exhibitions, archaeological exploration, translations, biographies and fiction.

The end of the fourth century when my story in this collection is set was a time of disintegration and dynamic change. While the classic periods of Rome are well recognised, the later one is not, and thus provides fertile ground for writers! *The Mystery of Victory* explores one of history's unanswered questions. It's also one of modern Roma Nova's foundation stories.

What are you writing at the moment?
The ninth book of the Roma Nova series, NEXUS, a novella featuring Aurelia Mitela, is with my editor. There will, of course, be revisions! NEXUS will appear in Autumn 2019.

How important is it for you to be part of a community of writers, and why?
Very important. Working with colleagues who are equally obsessed is refreshing and stimulating. Recently, at the Eboracum Roman Festival, the topic of death came up. I'm not sure what a normal person would have made of a group of writers, some dressed as Romans of various types, cheerfully and knowledgeably discussing who had the most deaths in their books and the various methods of dying, and not called the men in white coats.

Where can readers find out more about your books?
The usual retailers Amazon, Apple, Kobo, Barnes and Noble and good bookshops, but a good place to start is online at alison-morton.com. Readers can download *The Official Roma Nova Reading Guide* entirely free from online retailers and my website as a starting point.

The Invitation - Anthony Riches

'You're certain that you want to do this?'

Dubnus nodded, looking down the hillside at the walled settlement sprawling below them, where hundreds of roofs seemed to merge into one great, crouching entity.

'I did wonder if I'd be able to go through with it, but now I can see the city...' He blew out a long breath, staring down his tribe's capital. 'I know that I have to do this. To turn back now would be to spend the rest of my life wondering. Besides, Marcus, the invitation came from the king of my tribe. I can hardly ignore such a message.' He turned back to face his friend, smiling at the Roman's troubled expression. 'And there are people down there I haven't seen since I was forced to leave my people to be ruled by my father's usurper.'

'Do you really believe he wants to make peace with you? After fifteen years?'

The Briton nodded acceptance of the question's evident scepticism, one side of his mouth twisting up in unconscious recognition of his friend's continued disbelief of the invitation's sincerity.

'I know. It seems unlikely. And yet he will be all too well aware that the very act of raising his hand against a Roman centurion would be enough to see any man crucified, king or peasant. His entire family would be killed as an act of warning, and revenge.' He shrugged. 'Who knows what might be in his mind. Perhaps he is dying, and wishes to make peace before his exit from this world.'

'Perhaps.' Marcus shrugged. 'I suggest, in the absence of your being willing to take an escort in there with you, that you keep one hand on your axe handle at all times. You're completely sure you don't want anyone else to accompany you?'

'Utterly. I must walk in there with my head held up, regarding any man that cares to look at me with a stare that tells them I am still Dubnus, prince of the Brigantes, and that I will have the head off anyone who dares to challenge me.'

'Very well.' His brother officer shook his head in resignation. 'If that's your choice then you must follow that destiny, and see where it takes you. But be assured, if you have not emerged within a day, or given some sign of being the master of the situation, Rufius and I will bring our centuries in to find you, alive or dead, and in the doing of it put as many of those miserable Brits to the sword as we have to.'

Dubnus smiled again, hefting his axe.

'And in the event that you do come to retrieve my body, expect to find it surrounded by a good many others.'

The two men shared a moment of quiet amusement before the Briton nodded, turned away and headed down the hill towards his former home. Marcus watched him until he was halfway to the settlement's gates before walking away from the crest to join his own men, shaking his head in gentle disbelief at his friend's bravado.

He's set on doing it, I presume?'

The Roman nodded at the other officer who had accompanied them at the instruction of their cohort's first spear. His fellow centurion was, outwardly at least, well beyond the age when it was usual for a man to take his retirement and spend the remainder of his life in the relative luxury his wealth would afford.

'Of course he is, Rufius. When have you ever known the man to back away from anything that challenged him?'

The older man shrugged.

'It's his life to toss away as he chooses. I suggest we make camp, nice and obviously, set a double guard rota and get to sharpening our iron. You did promise him that his death would be suitably avenged?'

Marcus nodded gravely, recognising the deadly intent behind his friend's apparent levity.

'Of course.'

'In which case we could be wetting our blades soon enough. Your fool of a statue waver is offering good odds that someone down there will want to see our friend dead, and just this once

I'm finding it hard to disagree with him. If not because our brother officer is the rightful king of the tribe, then just because of the armour he wears. Prepare yourself never to see him again, at least not in this life.'

-x-

Dubnus strolled up to the gates of the Brigantes town with the purposeful gait of a man without the slightest concern for his own safety, looking down his nose at the two men who had been set to guard the gates. He pushed aside the glinting iron spear head that one of them had lifted to stop him, shaking his helmeted head in grim disapproval.

'Times must be hard, when my tribe raises spears against those that travel to its gates. And when its *warriors...*' he sneered at the youth whose spear he had batted aside. 'Are unwise enough to offer a blade to a centurion, alone or not.'

'Times *are* hard, Dubnus son of Cynbel.' The older of the pair, every inch as tall as the hulking centurion and no less blunt in his approach to a challenge, looked him up and down for a long moment before continuing. 'But not so hard that a son of the tribe, and a long-lost friend, cannot be greeted like the returning brother that he is. I don't know what prompted our king to summon you after so long living in the stone houses of the conquerors, but I welcome your return, my oldest friend.'

'And I accept your greeting, Morcant, *my* oldest friend. Are you still the best woodsman in the tribe?'

The two men embraced, while the younger guard watched coolly from his place by the gate.

'Not all will greet you so warmly, Centurion. I mean you no enmity, I simply speak the truth as I see it, as is the way-'

'The way of the Brigantes?' Dubnus shot him a hard grin, slapping his former friend on the shoulder before turning to face his younger companion. 'True enough, man-boy, my people always favoured the virtues of honesty and straight talking. Until the day that my father and I were attacked in the forest, by men whose preference was for a blade in the back. They came after us with five times our numbers to take the crown from their rightful king, and even if you are too young to have been present that day, perhaps your father was one of them. Perhaps you are the spawn of a man who murdered his king?'

'Perhaps you are a traitor to your people who deserves only-'

'Enough!' The older of the two raised a hand to his companion in warning. 'This is why I was set here alongside you, Aed, to ensure that our brother's first words with the tribe after fifteen winters were not to result in the airing of iron. The Dubnus I knew was only your age, when the tribe lost him, but even then he would have had the measure of you in a dozen heartbeats, were you rash enough to go blade to blade with him.'

The youth grinned hard at Dubnus, openly mocking him.

'And yet he ran from the tribe. And now he depends on the protection of his Roman iron, and the crest that marks him as a traitor.'

Morcant raised a hand in an unmistakable warning.

'And you, boy, risk your king's wrath. Our brother was invited here to make peace, and bring to an end the feud that has troubled our tribe since his father's murder. One more harsh word, *just* one, and I will act in anticipation of such justified anger and punish you myself!' He thrust the younger man away, putting a hand to the hilt of his own weapon in open threat, 'Will you make me do that?'

The youth returned his stare for a long moment before replying, shaking his head with an expression verging on surly.

'No. But his time will come.'

Dubnus smiled at him grimly, nodding.

'Indeed it will. As will yours. Everyone's time comes, boy, whether we choose to accept that fact or not. The trick is for a man to be ready, when Maponus calls for him, and to face his exit from this life with all the dignity he can muster. The dignity that my father was denied.'

He turned and walked away with Morcant at his side.

'You don't need me to show you the way to the king's hall, do you?'

Dubnus shook his head.

'I recall it as clearly as I did ten years ago. How could I not? I spent the first half of my life growing up in it, sucking at my mother's teat, playing with my father's dogs. My first sword...my first woman...'

An uneasy silence fell over the two men, Morcant looking across at his friend with the look of a man calculating how to tell him something he would not wish to hear. Dubnus shot him a glance, shaking his head at his friend's reticence.

'You can stop giving me the cow's eyes and get it over with. Who did Aife pair with, after my father was killed and I was forced to run to the Romans?'

'Judoc.'

Dubnus nodded, not faltering in his step for a moment as they walked down the long avenue, ignoring the hostile stares directed at him by the city's inhabitants.

'I was always aware of him watching her, from his place behind my father's throne. Indeed I often wondered if that was why he sided with the usurper's men, when the moment of betrayal was upon us'

Morcant nodded.

'You guessed well, friend. Judoc became the new king's champion, a position he holds to this day. And your woman was alone in the world, after her father's death alongside yours.'

'So she did what she had to do. I understand.'

'You will see her tonight, at the feast in your honour. Ready yourself for that, my brother, for she is no less beautiful than she was.'

Dubnus nodded

'I have been hardened in the fire of my service to Rome, Morcant. I went to the fortress on the hill an embittered boy, seeking blood and death, without concern for my own survival. But my centurion saw something in me that I could not discern for myself, and was patient and harsh at the same time. He taught me to live again, and to push away the pain until I no longer felt it. The Dubnus you knew is dead, brother, and in his place stands someone very different.'

Morcant stopped walking and looked at his former friend.

'That would be sad, were it entirely true. But I do not believe it, not as you tell it. You have changed, yes, in the same way that you wear that crested helmet as the symbol of your authority. But I see the Dubnus I lost ten winters ago now just as clearly as I saw him then. You are a warrior come of age, arrogant, brutal, and yes, a Roman...' he looked into Dubnus's eyes. 'But beneath all that you are still the man you were then. And that gives me joy, that your father's flame was not snuffed out completely. It still burns in you, my brother.'

-x-

'Axe, sword and dagger.'

The men guarding the hall's great wooden door stared at Dubnus in something close to open hostility, their leader holding out an open hand in a peremptory gesture.

'No.' He shook his head dismissively, sneering into their hostility. 'You will not disarm a centurion of Rome. For one thing, it is not permitted, and for another I will not have it.' He grinned hard at them, shaking his head as hands strayed nervously to the hilts of their weapons. 'Look at you, half a dozen men all fretting at the hilts of your swords at the sight of one man. Fucking cowards, all of you.'

The tribesmen bridled, but Dubnus simply shook his head and barked a laugh. 'You spineless bastards should have taken up arms in the war we have fought to defend you from the Selgovae, but instead you skulked here, like children hiding behind your mother's skirts, didn't you? And now it's too late. The Selgovae are vanquished...' he stepped forward to put himself less than a foot from their leader. 'And I have bathed in the blood that flew from this axe, as I strode among them like the warrior you pretend to be. I cheated death on that day, and invited Maponus to wait a little longer for my presence at his side, but if this is his day to summon me, I am ready to join him. So draw those swords, for all I care, and we shall see how many of you I can take with me.'

He leaned forward, putting a big finger on the other man's chest. 'I came in peace, at my king's request. I have sworn not to raise my iron to any man here unless I am challenged to do so. So either find the balls to challenge me, with the certainty of your death, either at my hands or on your king's command for attacking his invited guest, or get out of my way and let me pay my respects to him.'

The tribesman looked at Morcant.

'You will be responsible for his behaviour. If he causes us to draw these...' he tapped the hilt of his sword. 'Then you will share his fate.'

The Briton shrugged and nodded.

'And that would be the least I would owe him.'

The guards parted to allow the two men access, and Dubnus strode through them without a backward glance as they fell in close behind him. The king's hall was lit by the flames of dozens of tall candles, and at its far end was set the heavy oak chair that Dubnus's father had ordered to be carved, on inheriting the crown from his own father.

'He sits on the same chair?'

Morcant nodded.

'It was decided that the king would retain your father's throne, as a gesture of continuity.'

'Continuity of *what*? My father was murdered in the forest, shot by an honourless assassin as he fled from the slaughter of his bodyguard. What was there to *continue*?'

Morcant shrugged, keeping his voice low.

'The king's men portrayed your father's death as a tragic accident. He was to be celebrated, and remembered as a just and great ruler whose tradition would live on in his successor.'

Dubnus snorted a soft, derisive laugh

'But we know better, don't we, brother?'

He turned back to face the throne as the king's bodyguard walked out and took their places, two men before it and two behind, in the traditional manner. They were followed by a stately procession of the tribe's nobles, men he remembered well from his childhood, led by the man who had been his father's closest counsellor, the lord Haerviu. Locking stares with the oldest of the guards, standing in same place at the king's right shoulder that he had taken ten years before, Dubnus waited in silence as the king walked out and took his seat, arranging his ceremonial cloak across his legs before speaking. His voice was quiet in the near-empty hall, a faint echo reverberating from the wooden beams that arched over their heads.

'Welcome, Dubnus, son of Cynbel. In the years since your departure to live another life, far from our hall, our thoughts have often turned to you. Partly from the sadness of your loss to the tribe, after your father's tragic and untimely death. And partly with a sense of pride at your success in the world of the Romans. And now here you are, risen to the rank of centurion. You are to be congratulated, son of the tribe, for in some ways you have attained a status beyond anything you might have had here, had you stayed.'

Dubnus stepped forward and bowed stiffly, answering in the terms any centurion might have used under the same circumstances.

'King Seissyl, greetings to you. I have travelled from the fortress of stone on the windy hill in response to your invitation. I have come here in sure and certain knowledge that neither you nor any of your tribe will raise a hand against me without provocation, as is the way of these meetings between our two peoples.'

The king inclined his head in recognition of the point.

'And you have travelled wisely, son of the tribe, for you are under my express protection. Any man raising a hand against you will be declared outlaw.'

Dubnus bowed again.

'Thank you, king of the Brigantes tribe. And for my part I come in peace, and in the spirit of allowing the events that have led us both to come here as the men we are to go unstated. While I am an officer of Rome, and no longer subject to your rule, I choose to regard and respect your position as if I were still one of the tribe.'

The formalities and niceties observed, the king rose from his throne, gesturing for Dubnus to accompany him. From the surprised expressions on the faces of his nobles, Dubnus guessed that this was an unexpected departure from whatever they had been expecting.

'In which case I invite you to speak privately with me, Centurion, as one man of power to another. Although I would deem it a favour if you were to leave your axe with your boyhood friend. The sight of such a fearsome weapon is, I will admit, a little unnerving…under the circumstances.'

He smiled knowingly, and Dubnus, caught between outrage and amusement, took the middle path, handing the heavy bladed weapon to Morcant with a sardonic glance.

'Under the circumstances, King Seissyl, I can see why that might be the case.'

Following the king into his private rooms he found himself struck by the immediacy of his familiarity with both room and furnishings.

'It isn't just the throne you've kept as it was when my father was king?'

'Sit down, Dubnus.'

Seissyl's voice had lost its emollience, and was suddenly as hard-edged as Dubnus remembered from his time sitting quietly in the corner of the room, when his father had sought the counsel of his nobles before making major decisions for the tribe. He sat, waiting in silence as the king took his own chair, his smooth faced assurance replaced by something more urgent.

'I don't have long to speak with you alone, not if the men who seek to control me are not to start wondering as to my purpose in calling you here. I told them that I wanted to make peace with the son of the man they killed to put me on the throne, now that you are in such a position of influence. But your invitation here has a deeper purpose than simply seeking to reconcile you to the tribe - although that would be welcome enough, were it possible.'

Dubnus leaned back in his chair.

'Reconciliation? Why would you even try? It might have been ten years ago, but I can still recall with total clarity the weight of my father's dying body leaning on me, as I half-carried him away from the men who had dealt him that death wound. I recall their shouts of triumph at seeing the arrow that pierced his back, as we fled from the swords that had already killed those of his bodyguard who remained loyal. I remember most clearly of all the voice of the man who put that arrow into his king's back, and his shout of joy as my father stumbled and cried out with the pain as it pierced his body.'

'And yet you can be assured that I had no part in your father's murder.' Dubnus stared back at the king in silence. 'I know you are hardly inclined to accept the statement, but look into my eyes and gauge the truth of my words. I was the most loyal of the king's men, and horrified when Haerviu told me of the true manner of Cynbel's death.'

'And yet here you are, wearing his crown.'

'And what was I to do, when my fellow nobles selected me to take his place? He had grown too close to Rome, they told me, and had to be removed from the throne for the good of the tribe. They said that it was with regret that they took his life, and sought to take yours too.' Seissyl shook his head. 'I believed them, Dubnus, believed in their sincerity, and I took the throne with as great a show of reluctance as possible, promising to retain everything that was good about Cynbel's rule. But I soon enough perceived the unhappy reality of my fellow nobles' failings.'

'Their cowardice in the face of war?'

The king nodded.

'I was already sorely disappointed with their behaviours, even before the Selgovae came south with fire and iron to plunder our lands even as they sought to drive you from them, while my lords advised – insisted - that we do nothing to assist your struggle. It soon became clear that they expected me to reward them for placing me on the throne by turning a blind eye to their abuses of the power they held. Haerviu sought an audience with me, and practically ordered me to dismiss the complaints against them, leaving them free to punish those they had already wronged for being unwise enough to seek justice. If I failed to favour them in this way, it was implied, they would be forced to take the same action against me that was Cynbel's fate. I would die, and my entire family would suffer the same fate, once they had ceased serving whatever purposes could be found for them after my death. After all, they told me, what regicide ever leaves his victim's family alive to seek revenge?'

Dubnus nodded slowly.

'And so it is that you have invited me here, on the face of it as an errant son of the tribe from whom you seek some degree of reconciliation. Whereas in reality you have summoned me as a centurion, to save you from the threat of your own murder. You wish to avoid the fate my father suffered. And the irony of my being the instrument you seek to use for that purpose is not lost on me, as you can imagine.' He stared impassively at the waiting king. 'So why, tell me, should I lift even a finger to assist you? What difference would it make to me whether you lived or died, *King* Seissyl?'

The other man shrugged.

'Little enough, I'd imagine. Why should you care who rules the tribe, now that you are a centurion, and side with the conquerors who govern our lives? But perhaps you should consider the realities of what my death would mean, and the opportunity that my request for assistance provides to you.'

The burly centurion pursed his lips, keeping his face stone like in its immobility.

'Go on.'

'If I die, then my killers will select another man to take my place. A man who will be equally beholden to them, and in their thrall. The injustices will continue unchecked. Theft. Rape. Murder. Your people will suffer at the hands of the men they expect to govern them fairly and wisely.'

'Whereas?'

'If you kill just one man for me, I am as sure as I can be that the rest will buckle at the threat that you...*that Rome*...will come for them too. I need you to kill Haerviu, here, today, in front of his fellow nobles. With the leader of this pack of dogs on a pyre, my bodyguard will be able to face down the rest of them, freed of the naked threat he holds over them and their families.'

'You *know* that they will be loyal?'

'Judoc has sought their commitment, one man at a time and with a knife ready for any that refuse, and, one by one, they have sworn their loyalty if they are free to exercise it.'

'Judoc...'

'I know. He stood at your father's back as a younger man, and yet betrayed him in the forest, taking his sword to his fellow bodyguards and leaving Cynbel open to attack. But he did not do so from choice.'

'He says he was coerced?'

'I know he was. Haerviu has admitted as much. He played a clever game ten years ago, just as he does now. Just as he is the worst of my nobles in his behaviour to his subjects, he is the most devious and calculating of them. Shorn of his leadership they will fall into line under my men's blades.'

'Judoc took my woman, once I was out of the way.'

'He saved Aife from being used for sport by Haerviu and his cronies. When they went to her dead father's house to prey on his daughter, Judoc was faster, and was there to meet them with the news that he had claimed her in marriage. But for that, her life would have been both short and ugly from that moment.'

Dubnus nodded slowly, and the king leaned forward with his hand outstretched.

'There is no question that you have the power to dispense this justice on the behalf of a king who requests Rome's assistance. And in doing so you can be the man who persuades the king of the Brigantes to take a side in any future resumption of the war with the northern tribes. The question is, will you?'

'Yes…' Dubnus waited until his response was reflected in Seissyl's look of relief before continuing. 'But this is not a one-sided transaction. Not even a king gets have justice meted out on his behalf without paying some price for it.'

'And your price is?'

'The head of the man who betrayed my father. Promise me that, and I will do as you wish. Refuse me and you will have to deal with this problem of your own making without my assistance. It's your choice.'

-x-

'My lords, the king!'

Seissyl swept back into the room and headed for his throne with the dark face of a man who had been thwarted, while Dubnus strolled in his wake, stopping next to Haerviu and glancing casually at him before speaking, his vine stick ostentatiously held in both hands.

'The king seems a little less than delighted with the result of our discussion, wouldn't you agree?'

The noble smiled slowly, nodding as his ruler slumped onto the carved wooden chair with the look of a beaten man.

'The king failed to convince you to do his bidding, I presume. That was his purpose in inviting you here, wasn't it? The support of a Roman centurion, and perhaps a judicial murder as well. Revenge for you, relief for him…?'

Dubnus turned to look at him, his face an expressionless mask.

'As a Roman centurion I am bound to ask you exactly what it is that you're implying?'

The noble smiled, his eyes hard and untouched by humour.

'Of course you are. You're Cynbel's son alright, with the same big-balled arrogance. So you can't comment as a centurion, but perhaps you can as a *son of the tribe*? Don't forget that your former love is still very much within my grasp, Dubnus, wife of the king's champion or not.'

'Seissyl wasn't wrong about you, was he?'

'No. He wasn't. I rule this tribe, using the king as a puppet. Rome deals with me, or not at all.'

Dubnus shrugged.

'In that case I can be as frank as you like.' Seissyl was speaking to Judoc, shaking his head and raising his hand in a gesture of negation. 'The king asked me to dispense justice on behalf of the empire. I pointed out to him that I was invited here not as a Roman, but as a warrior of the Brigantes tribe.'

'Which means that you can't do as he wishes?' Haerviu's mile broadened. 'So his effort to turn Rome against his own people has failed.'

'Yes. Of course as a Brigantes I was willing to consider his request all too seriously.' Dubnus fixed his gaze on Judoc. 'After all, you did have my father killed. I told him I'd kill you, here and now, in return for the one life I crave most of all.'

The noble followed Dubnus's stare, nodding as he saw the bodyguard return it, cold eyed.

'And obviously he refused to bargain with you. The death of the leader of his guards would leave him dangerously exposed just at the time when he needs their swords to cow my fellow nobles.'

The centurion stretched both arms out, rolling his shoulders.

'That's a reasonable assumption.'

He pivoted at the waist to swing the stick one handed into Haerviu's throat with all the strength in his body, dropping the impromptu weapon and drawing his sword and dagger simultaneously. The noble staggered backwards, clutching at the vitis's point of impact, the only sound in the shocked hall's silence the gargling splutter of his choking struggle to breathe through his closing windpipe. The man around him scattered, reaching for their swords while Dubnus stared down the length of his gladius at them.

'*Hold!* Your king commands it! Rome has dispensed justice to a traitor, and at my request! Put down your weapons, if you wish to avoid his fate!'

Seissyl gestured to his guards, and Judoc led them forwards with swords raised to disarm Haerviu's dithering followers. Dubnus sheathed his weapons, tucked his vine stick into his ornately decorated belt and strolled over to where Morcant stood, open mouthed, the axe hanging from one hand, completely forgotten.

'I'll be needing that.'

His friend nodded, holding out the weapon, then reeled as the stone-faced centurion jabbed the weapon's heavy iron head into his face, sending blood jetting from his nostrils as his nose shattered. Hooking the axe's blade behind his ankle Dubnus pulled savagely, whipping the leg out from beneath his stricken victim and dumping him to the stone floor. Stepping forward, he put the axe's blade to his friend's throat and pinned him in place with a booted foot, speaking conversationally to the men surrounding him.

'You men watching might consider what I've just done to be unmanly. First Haerviu, and now Morcant, and neither of them given any chance to fight back.' He looked over at the noble's contorted body, nodding as his first victim fought a losing battle against the asphyxiation that was killing him, then down at Morcant as he spat a mouthful of blood and shattered teeth across the boot that had him captive. 'If you move before I'm done talking I'll hack both your arms off and leave you to the mercy of the tribe. Got that?'

'Y…yes.'

'Very well.' Dubnus switched his attention to his horrified audience. 'As to my lack of honour in dealing with these two murderers, I learned it all from you, my brothers of the tribe. On the day that my father died with an arrow in his back I swore to take revenge that Cynbel's killers would never see coming. And so it was that I agreed to kill Haerviu at your king's request. I would have done it anyway, given he was the man who ordered my father's death, but my agreement was that I got to take another life as my payment. The life of Cynbel's killer.'

He looked at Judoc for a moment, nodding hard faced respect at the man.

'Our king thought I wanted you, but the truth is that you're not the man that killed my father. Yes, you betrayed him along with many other men, but you weren't the one who tracked our hunting party through the forest and guided the killers to us. And then, when his bodyguard sold their lives dearly to give him the chance to escape, you weren't the man who put an arrow into his back. Both of those acts of treachery were committed by a skilled hunter. The tribe's most skilled hunter. *Him.*'

He gestured down at Morcant.

'This bastard led the killers to us, and then when it seemed as if we were going to escape their attack, it was him that killed his king, even if the arrow took two more days and a night to finish its work. He'd have killed us both on the spot too, if not for the fact that we were so close to the river when the ambush was sprung, and managed to leap into it and be carried away before our pursuers could reach the bank.' He looked down at his friend with an expression of loathing. 'And now you're wondering how long I've known, aren't you?'

He leaned forward and stared into the battered face.

'Since the moment that arrow struck Cynbel, *that*'s how long I've known you betrayed us. I heard your shout of triumph as you saw the arrow hit home, the same shout you always gave when you put an arrow into a deer. In the early days, while I was only a soldier and adapting to life with the Romans, I was desperate to get at you with a blade, so desperate that my centurion had me beaten more than once for trying to get out of the fortress to come here and find you. He told me something I've lived by ever since, when I was hanging from the whipping post the second time and he'd threatened me with death if I did it a third time. He told me that revenge is a far more satisfying meal if you let it cool first. You must have been shit scared at first, when it got back to the tribe that I'd survived and was in service with the Romans, but over the years you came to believe that you'd got away with it, didn't you? You got complacent. So complacent that you never saw my revenge coming until it was an axe head in your face.'

He stepped back, hefting the axe in readiness to strike.

'You can get up and die like a man, or you can lie there and I'll behead you where you lie. You choose.'

After a moment Morcant rolled onto his front, pushing himself up onto his knees and then standing, turning to face Dubnus with a snarl of hate on his ruined face.

'I did it for Aife! I always loved her, and Haerviu-'

The axe swung in a blurred arc and struck with a slapping crunch of severed bone, Morcant's head bouncing once before rolling away into the shadows, while his decapitated corpse stood stock still for a moment with blood pumping from its severed arteries before crumpling to the floor. Dubnus twisted the weapon's shaft, flicking blood across the watching nobles' finely woven tunics.

'Save your story for the ferryman. Doubtless he's heard a thousand just the same.' Dubnus smirked at the blood spattered nobles, swinging the heavy axe onto his shoulder. 'And how very apt, that you traitors should bear the mark of my revenge. Keep those tunics just as they are, my lords, and let them remind you of what will happen to you if your king dies unexpectedly.'

He turned to Seissyl, bowing deeply.

'Your request for Rome's assistance has been answered, king of the Brigantes. Can I tell my superiors that the tribe will stand alongside Rome, if ever the northern tribes decide to renew their insurrection?'

The king nodded, his face still white at the speed and savagery with which his will had been enacted.

'You may.'

Very well. You can expect more Romans to attend upon you to negotiate the terms of a new treaty with that as the central object. They will be officers senior to me, indeed they will the sort of gentlemen you will be more comfortable with than a hard-eyed killer like me, I expect, but never doubt that I will return to handle the more practical side of negotiations if necessary. But for now my presence here is no longer necessary, and I see no point in provoking your people with my presence any further, especially as any attempt to kill me will result in the destruction of this settlement and the deaths of everyone in it.'

He drew his dagger from the scabbard on his belt.

'Which leaves just one more practicality to be dealt with, before I leave.'

-X-

'Centurion Two Knives!'

Marcus turned away from his contemplation of a book he'd brought with him from the fortress's library, allowing the scroll to curl up as he got to his feet and strode to the hill's crest, from where his watch officer's alert had been shouted. Rufius joined him as he crossed the camp that was still in the process of being carved out of the soft soil.

'Surely he can't be coming out already. He's barely had the time to get his first dozen insults out!'

A figure was climbing the hill's slope, the crested helmet a clear giveaway as to his identity. Both men stood and waited as their friend laboured up the last hundred paces of the climb, Rufius shaking his head in disbelief.

'I was sure you weren't coming out of there with your head still attached to your neck.'

Dubnus stopped in front of them, breathing hard from the climb, and shook his head dismissively.

'It was simple enough. The king wanted Rome's support, I gave it to him in return for a small favour of my own, and our business was done.'

Marcus drew breath to comment, but Morban, who had hurried across from his duties in their wake, beat him to it.

'That's all very well, Dubnus, but there are important questions to be answered!'

'Such as, statue waver?'

The signifier ignored the testy tone in Marcus's voice.

'Such as, Centurion sir, the circumstances of our comrade's business down there.' He hooked a thumb over his shoulder at the camp behind him. 'There are a lot of men back there with a personal interest in that.'

'None of their interests quite as deep as your own, eh Morban? I always said you'd offer the odds on who could piss up a tent pole the highest, given the chance.' Dubnus rolled his eyes at his old sparring partner from the days when they had been chosen man and standard bearer in the same century. 'So what do you want to know?'

'You're going to humour this idiot's money making schemes?'

The big Briton winked at Rufius, then turned back to Morban, grinning at the suspicion in the older man's eyes.

'You know I survived, so that's one half of your customers leaving their coin in your purse. What else were you taking odds on?'

'How many men you killed down there. Wait a minute…'

The standard bearer frowned at something he'd just realised.

'A few of your boys put their money on you coming back with the blood of two men on your hands. Good sized stakes as well. I nearly turned them away, but…'

'But you're too greedy, aren't you?'

Morban stared at his friend with growing horror.

'I've got ten in gold riding on that number. And now here you are, with blood on your armour…'

'And these.'

Dubnus tossed a pair of severed ears into the standard bearer's hands, Morban catching them reflexively before realising what they were.

'Gods below! Did you have to-'

'Prove what I'd done to a distrustful tight-arse like you? Yes. You would never have paid out without them. So, there you have it. Two kills. It's time to cough the coin up, Morban!'

The standard bearer turned and trudged away, white-faced with the shock of his loss but knowing that he had little alternative but to pay out a modest sized fortune to the men who had placed successful bets, whether he suspected they had been assisted to their choice of wager or not.

'So what actually happened?'

Dubnus shrugged wearily at Marcus.

'I killed one man for the king, and the other for myself. Both of them had a part in my father's death, both of them had it coming. Neither of them realised what was going to happen until it hit him.'

'And how does revenge taste?'

The Briton shook his head.

'Nowhere near as good as you'd imagine, brother. As you'll discover some day for yourself, when you catch up with the men who murdered your own father.'

The Roman nodded.

'But you'd do it again, wouldn't you?'

His friend thought for a moment.

'Yes. Because when it came down to it, I didn't do it to make myself feel better. It doesn't bring my father back across the river, or give me back the woman I lost, or mend the grief I suffered from being betrayed by my closest friend. And it won't give you any pleasure either, when your time for revenge comes. I did it because it was right.'

He stretched, rolling his head on his broad shoulders.

'I knew the two men I needed dead, if I were to give my father's spirit, and I watched them both die with a prayer to tell him that he was avenged at last.'

Rufius put his hand on the big man's shoulder.

'Well done, brother. Very well done. Tonight we'll crack open that amphora of wine we dragged along and raise a cup in his name.'

Dubnus nodded wearily, smiling at the prospect.

'Sounds like a fitting end to the day. But before that, however, and before I allow drink to befuddle my wits, you'll have to excuse me. I'm going to confiscate my boys' winnings until they get the chance to spend them on something more fruitful than whatever nonsense bet Morban comes up with to claim back his losses.'

He stalked away in pursuit of the standard bearer, and his comrades watched him go, Marcus's face tight with emotion.

'He makes it all sound so simple, doesn't he? Two men dead, revenge taken, no repercussions.' Rufius shook his head in admiration. 'But it's one thing to take justice in a tribal village, and another to do it in the greatest city in the world. And the men who killed your father won't be as easy to find, or to kill.'

'I know.' Marcus ran a hand through his hair. 'But you heard what he said. It didn't make him feel any better. It didn't mend his grief. But it did feel right.'

Interview with Anthony Riches

What is it about Rome that inspires you?

I genuinely don't really know. I like to read thrillers and Sci-fi, and most definitely not historical fiction, so why Rome is a mystery to me, to be honest. That said I do love to touch history, and Rome's achievements were so grand that there's plenty of them left to stand and stare at (and sometimes touch). Go to the Colosseum and get on the underground tour to know what I mean. The whole place was a great big machine designed to process fifty thousand victims a year (but in the context of a very organised and lucrative business) for the entertainment of the city's population. If that's not fascinating and horrifying in equal measure as a gauge of just what Rome was, I don't know what is. And therein lies the 'allure' - a continent spanning empire that was in reality no better than the biggest and nastiest street gang (for a long time) in the known world. Like I said, horribly fascinating.

What inspired you to write this particular story?

I stood on Hadrians' Wall, in the remains of a Hadrianic era fort called Housesteads (the Hill, in my Empire series) in the pouring rain one summer day in 1996 and was struck by what a culture shock the place – and the entire country - must have been for the average Roman. After that I had a problem, which is one that's gifted/afflicted me since boyhood, the inability to stop imagining the 'next scene'. Sometimes a piece of dialogue or action will torment me for weeks, until I give up and write it down – at which point the next scene, which may or may not be directly related to the last one, comes along to start the process again. With 'Wounds of Honour', as with a couple of other manuscripts, I gave in and wrote the story down. For a while, as I refined my abilities to write mass market fiction, this was more about the fascinating research potential of the Roman empire in the late 2nd century, but as I got better at dialogue, and showing rather than telling, this faded into the background and was replaced by the genuine pleasure of creating characters whose story and actions came to populate the world I was imagining. The only downside of this whole process is that these characters sometimes do things which are very contrary to the ideas I started out with...

Can you tell us about your other work inspired by Rome?

I've written ten books in the Empire series (a planned 25 book series tracking the vivid and bloody history of the late 2nd/early 3rd centuries through the eyes of Marcus Valerius Aquila, a fugitive from imperial persecution turned war hero), and additionally a trilogy entitled 'The Centurions' which tells the story of the Batavian Revlot of AD69 that shook the empire to its foundations and very nearly removed northern Europe from Roman control.

What do you enjoy most about writing?

That magic moment when the characters you think you know suddenly decide to do something completely unplanned - like get themselves unexpectedly killed! Some of my most illuminative moments have been sitting back and mouthing the words 'surely not?' (or more likely 'wtf?') to myself.

If you were transported back to the time your story is set, who is the first person you would want to talk to and why?

The emperor Commodus, to find out whether he was really the waste of space that he's been written up as by the received version of history. After all, it's the victors that right the history.

What would you bring back from ancient Rome with you?

In one hand, a handful of coins. Really rare gold aureii minted by 'gone before you knew it' emperors like Galba, Vitellius, Pertinax, etc, which will be worth (literally) a mint! Yes, I am a mercenary. And in the other hand, I'd be carrying an imperial legion standard, although quite how I'd get it off the specimen of military pride carrying it, I have no idea.

If there was one event in the period you could witness (in perfect safety) what would it be?

Doubtless people are going to respond to this with scenes like 'the death of Julius Caesar', or 'the suicide of Mark Anthony'. I'm less classically inclined. I'm tempted to opt for the defence of the Pons Sublicius bridge by One Eyed Horatius Cocles in 508BC, which is now thought to be 1st century BC Republican propaganda to cover up for fact that the army actually ran away and allowed the Etruscans to take the city unchallenged (let's face it, the Victorians probably got fed a lot of the same fare about events hundreds of years before that showed Britain in a less than glorious light), and Livy thought the whole thing was preposterous (Horatius is supposed to have swum the Tiber in armour, an almost guaranteed death sentence). But my actual choice would be to find out what really happened when Vespasian's son-in-law, the victorious general Cerialis, faced off to the Batavian leader Julius Civilis, across a severed bridge at the end of that tribe's revolt (as imagined in 'Betrayal', 'Onslaught' and 'Retribution'). Pardon? Execution? Exile? We'll probably never know, as the account we have, written by Tacitus, literally ends at that moment (the monk copying it presumably having been killed by a Viking).

Why do you think readers are still so thirsty for stories from this period?

A thousand years of history (we don't all live in the 1st century AD), a continent spanning empire...gladiators, legions, barbarians, glorious enemies like the Parthians...what's not to love?

What are you writing at the moment?

Book 11 in the Empire series - set in the emperor's province of Aegyptus, where all is not well - as yet untitled.

Where can readers find out more about your books?

Have a look at my website, http://www.anthonyriches.com for more details of the stories that force their way out of my head when I'm not reading about fast cars and modern warfare, reading thrillers and sci-fi and, just to add to the fun, working at a very challenging and entertaining day job!

Exiles - Antonia Senior

The poet eases his tongue into her mouth. He probes. She lets him. He pulls back, and she can see his eyes, watery and squid-ink dark. She closes hers, and presses her lips together into a thin line.

'How strange,' she hears him say. 'How strange you are.'

He puts his wrinkled, old man hands on her.

In he comes again, his tongue tip-tapping at her teeth. She lets it in, feeling him push deeper. He finds the puckered stump, licking at it. She feels it all the way down to her toes. His tongue swirls fatly in that space where her phantom tongue lies - the ghostly part of her that itches and twitches, and probes her teeth for trapped spinach, and when she forgets, so rarely now, wraps itself around silent consonants.

'I remember you,' he says. 'I remember when it happened.'

She nods and opens her eyes so that he can see her sadness. He was always in and out of the house, laughter and glamour snapping at his heels. A treasured guest. An adornment - like a precious vase, or a giant eel, or a thick necklace hung with glossy amethysts.

The poet. Never a neutral epithet.

'Look, there goes Ovid, the poet,' said Agrippina when they were little and he was young. The way she said it, the word was a sneer. 'Look, there goes the poet,' said Agrippina's sister Julia, and the way she said it the word was a hymn, an offering. His art was the bridge to the divine. There they were then, the first time she had seen him, peering into a world of adults around the corner of a hedge. Watching the poet spin his lattice of stories, and throw it high and wide above the silent, upturned faces. Watching them caught and tied.

The garden was thick with golden torch-light and the smell of the dusk-drunk roses.

And even then she thought, when is a story a story and when is it just a lie?

The girls' mother Julia was there, chief among the worshipers.

Little Julia had her mother's face, that sweet oval which tapered down to a pointed chin. They listened to the poet in the same rapt haze, hands clasped. They loved a story. How did they feel later, when their own lives became stories, distorted and told and retold? Stories and lies. Lies and stories.

She had a tongue then. She had said to Agrippina: Your Mother loves him, mistress. Your sister, too. Look.

'Oh, that woman loves poets,' said Agrippina. 'And my sister is a simpleton. But look at my Father.'

She looked, then, at Agrippa. He was restless. Bored. His eyes flickered around the garden, looking for diversion. He caught sight of them suddenly, peering out from behind the hedge. We will be in trouble, she thought, her stomach sinking. But he had smiled, softening that square, Saturnine face. He had winked at them both. He died not long after. The wink was the last thing either had from him. That one, silent snap of an eyelid.

The poet's voice, loud and sonorous, sang on.

No. That can't be right. Agrippina was a toddler when Agrippa died. She is confusing two different days. Even the stories our memories tell us are tricky and full of lies. Agrippa's wink came earlier, much earlier. She has hoarded it. The day she is thinking of, the first time she saw the poet, it must have been Agrippina's step-father, Tiberius, who sat there with an irascible face. He hated the modern poets, particularly this one. He thought poems should be formal and full of divine fire. Yes, he hated this poet, and his playful obsession with love and mortal life in all its beauty and ugliness.

Tiberius then. Sitting in Rome waiting for everybody he hates to die.

#

That was then, and here he is now. The shining chronicler of sex and love. He is almost unrecognisable. Young, he was not a handsome man. But he was violently attractive - adored for his wit and his joy and his irreverence. What is left? White stubble and the wrinkled skin of a man who was once portly and is now despairingly thin. The misery buzzing round him like a cloud of flies. His voice is a quavering, unused thing. She feels something akin to pity, and drives it off.

Poor child, he is saying. 'You poor child. Oh, she was always difficult your little Mistress. Even as a child. A little girl with the face of a nymph and the eyes of a Gorgon. She was always watching. Silent like you. But I remember you. Those eyebrows! Or rather, that eyebrow. Even our faces can tell a story.'

He runs a finger the wrong way across her eyebrow, which sits squarely across her forehead. The hair bristles. She does not like it, and she has to work hard to keep her face passive. She seeks to distract him, and raises her head, catching his finger in her tongueless mouth. She watches his eyes widen and the quick bob of the apple in his neck as he swallows.

#

Later, he collapses onto her. She worries for a minute that he might be dead. His head is buried in her armpit.

He is alive, just. He shouts into her armpit: 'Oh, you smell of Rome!'

She doubts it. She was weeks on a boat getting here. Her skin is streaked with puke and salt and the bosun's slobber.

'Yes,' he says. 'Of Rome! The women here chew a root they pick from the swamp. Chew chew chew. Like cows. They smell of aniseed. They open their great, stupid barbarian mouths to speak their barbaric Greek, and a Roman could near faint with it. The smell of it gets into their skin and their hair. I asked a girl about it. She said she couldn't smell it. There she was, reeking of goat's milk and aniseed, and she couldn't smell it. She had no idea. Can you believe it?'

She pulls the appropriate face from her repertoire and wears it. He lifts his head from her armpit, and looks at her face. 'Yes,' he says. 'Yes.'

He rolls away from her. 'Oh, everything here smells different. The houses smell of different bricks. The wine. The oil. The cheese. Oh, the horrible cheese. The oil in the lamps smells of fish. Do you understand? And the worst of it is that I am beginning to forget what Rome smells like. I know this is all wrong. But I can't remember the right. I can't.'

Don't cry old man, she thinks, fighting to keep her eyes from rolling. She strokes his arm, and kisses his shoulder.

He falls silent, eyes watery. He looks down at her, pats her on the head like a docile child.

'The letter you brought,' he says. 'From Agrippina. Did you read it?'

She shakes her head. Makes her stupid face.

'Can you read?'

She shakes her head again. Sad face.

He claps his hands, calling for his slave. She makes to rise out of the bed, but he holds her arm. 'Stay', he says. The slave is ordered to bring wine and food, and to stoke the brazier higher. It is cold beyond the bed, so very cold. She huddles in to him when the slave is gone, pushing herself against him like a cat.

He pats her head and he pulls the heavy furs higher.

'I have never known cold like it,' he says. 'This is only the start. I have done two winters now. It gets into my bones. My bones are made of ice. And the worst of it, is that when the river freezes, the raiders come. You must be out before it freezes, little one. They ride across the ice on those horrible, little shaggy ponies. Like centaurs. Shaggy, furry, ugly barbarians on shaggy, furry horses. Like centaurs from a bad epic. Oh, you should hear them. They whoop and they scream. They fire their arrows. I had a girl, here. Last winter. She walked near the wall. An arrow came from the sky, looping up and over. They come all the time, thwacking into the ground, the roofs. This one just nicked her arm. But they poison them you know. Her arm blew up. Skin like an angry drum. She wept and cried. All the offerings could not save her. The fever took her.'

She shivers. The poet looks pleased. He watches her to see how the words affect her.

'Her arm was striped with purples and yellows, radiating out from the cut like a web. She lost her smatter of Greek at the end. Babbled in a stream of mad consonants. People die in the language they hear at their birth. I will die in Latin, even if they bury my bones here, in this treeless, flat wasteland.'

He grips her by the shoulders, forces her to look into his eyes. His fingers dig into her skin, scraping at her with his too-long nails. He says it again. 'I do not want to die here, screaming in Latin. None of them speak Latin. Oh, don't look at me like that. I understand the irony.'

He lets her go, cross with her. She must not let her face slip. Stupid. She slumps back into the pillow.

He mutters: 'I do not want to die here shouting to an empty room. Here, I am voiceless.'

She thinks: I will die silently.

#

She wakes. The brazier has died. There is cold blue light filtering through the edge of the heavy curtains. She slips out of the bed, and the shock of the freezing air is like a punch. She uses the pot, then walks to the window, feeling the goosebumps rise. She pulls back the edge and looks out. They are high up in this room, and she can see out and over the wall towards the grey sea. The sky is a giant thunder-cloud waiting to rage. The ship will not be leaving today, she thinks.

She hears him behind her using the pot, grumbling about the uselessness of the slave and the brackishness of the water, and the cold, Oh Gods, the cold.

Was it exile that made him peevish, she wonders? Or is it age? How can men bear it, she wonders. What God's trick is it, that the longer men live the more irascible they become? Why would each passing year make you angrier, rather than more at peace?

Behind her, the irritations continue. Is he talking to her, or to himself? Perhaps this is the exile's morning ritual, the same each day, like a Priest at the altar of Discontent.

Perhaps, Julia the Younger is the same on that island of hers. Perhaps, there, she whines of the heat and the salt and the silence and the surrounding sea. Or perhaps she is more stoical than her erstwhile friend, who grumbles and whines like a child. Men had to invent a philosophy and call it Stoicism; women are born knowing how to endure.

She is cold, and the smile cannot be put off any longer. She

111

fixes it on, and she turns back to him. He stops his grumbling, and looks at her. In his silent stare, she feels the power of her smile and her young, supple body. She is 27 to his 53.

Sweet girl, the poet says. Come here.

Afterwards he says. 'The letter. The letter from Agrippina. She says that He is softening. People have been working for me. My wife. She knows Livia, you know. My dear wife,' he says, his hand lying like a dead toad on her skin. She longs to push it off.

'Are my poems helping?' he asks her. He has been sending letters home, full of poetry. Beautifully written of course. He is not capable of writing inelegantly. But so *embarrassing*. Anguished appeals for clemency from the Divine ruler. Long tributes to the man who exiled him here, interspersed with long, elegant whining about being here. The Whine Cycle they are calling it back home, in the fashionable salons. At Agrippina's last party, she had watched silently from the shadows as one of the poet's letters from Tomis was read out to general mirth. Didn't the Athenians laugh at exiled Alcibiades, sitting in bleak Sparta eating his black broth?

There is, among the fashionable set, an appreciation of Augustus' hitherto unsuspected sense of the ironic. Sending this poet to this place? Brilliant, darling. Just too perfect!

Oh, yes, they laughed as they read of the cold, and the ranging barbarians, and the houses made of straw. They patted their silk robes, and drank their expensive reds, and flirted with one another ceaselessly.

Was his wife at that party? If she was, she had been laughing too.

He is looking at her. Eyes, big and pleading. 'Are they helping?' he asks again.

She nods. Smiles.

He smiles back, and the hope in his face makes her pause. It makes her feel troubled.

'Do you know what I really miss the most? My garden. My orchard. I worked it myself, you know. The soil in my hands. Trying out phrases on the worms, the birds. And I wrote beneath the fruit trees. I knew myself to be happy, I could not understand how happy until now. It takes misery to understand past happiness.'

She nods. This, she agrees with.

Perhaps he sees something sincere in her face, because he kisses her. 'Come now,' he says. 'I must work. Leave me. Come later, though? You will come later?'

She nods, and slips out of the room.

#

There is nothing funny about this place when you are here. She borrows some heavy furs and walks around. It does not take long. There are baths, of sorts, and temples. It is not quite as bleak as The Poet would have his friends back home believe. But then, she is not imprisoned here, she supposes.

In Greek, Tomis means pieces. The Poet had told her that the name derives from one of the crimes of Medea. Fleeing her father, she landed on this shore. When her father's chasing sail was seen, she sought a diversion. She killed her brother, and chopped him into fragments. The father was forced to look for and assemble all the pieces of his son before he could resume the chase for his daughter.

She shivers. She thinks of Augustus, who turned his furious wrath on his faithless daughter, Julia - her erstwhile mistress. He exiled her, too, to a small island in the sea. And then the same punishment for Julia's son, and her daughter, the younger Julia. Isn't exile a kind of tearing of a person's being? A chopping up of the living soul, so that a fragment lives at home, and a fragment in the place of exile, and all the other pieces flailing between the two? She stands on the wall, and looks out over the flat, treeless scrubland. I was cut in real pieces, she thinks, remembering the pain. So fuck the poet, and his broken soul.

#

She makes her face sweet that evening. She fills his wine cup, again and again, even though he protests. I'm not a big drinker, he says. No more. No more. But she smiles and trills and fusses him.

The night draws in. She sits closer, fluttering at him. Listening to him talk and talk.

At last, he says: 'Augustus.'

She listens.

'I hate him. I hate him. Oh, it eats me. All that hypocritical shit about other people's sex lives, when everyone knows he is a goat. And sending me here. I hate him. I fight to keep it out of the poems, but it seeps in, like poison.'

She keeps her face light and sweet and trusting.

'You know why he sent me here? Not for poems which were years old. They were the pretence. Oh, the old goat is good at pretence. I knew things, you see. I knew that Julia the Younger was whispering. I knew she was fighting the rise of Tiberius, and who can blame her. Odious man. I knew. And I whispered, too.'

She strokes his face, her palm catching on that silver stubble. He is pleased with himself. He wants to tell someone, wants to make himself the heart of a story which isn't really about him. Come on, old man. Tell.

'I passed the word between the plotters,' he says, his voice a whisper in the empty room. 'We were close. So close. To wrecking Tiberius, and rescuing Julia's little brother Agrippa Posthumus from his island. Her brother with his Julian blood.'

His voice falls lower. He strokes her eyebrow. 'Your brother,' he says.

She flinches. She can't help it. He opens his arms and she falls in to them. She takes the comfort on offer, breathing his skin, feeling him stroke her hair. She wants to tell him stories, too. Wants to tell him what it felt like when Agrippina demanded she be punished. When Agrippina screamed - she's a filthy slave. She keeps calling herself my sister. Just because my father ploughed a filthy slave does not make her my sister.

She wants to tell him about how Tiberius ordered it. How they held her down. How the knife cut, and her mouth filled and frothed and how she was choking and spluttering and screaming through her own blood. She wants to tell her story, too. But she

114

can't.

#

She is back in Rome, at last. She walks around, gleefully seeking out Roman smells. The resin of the pine trees. The musk of the wine. The scented lemon perfume she rubs into her skin. The oil in the lamps which smells of oregano and olives.

She has her eyebrow plucked. She lies too long in the hot bath, thinking of how cold it was in Tomis. She has her slave remove all the hair on her body, and dress her hair.

She goes to see her real master. Her new master. The Emperor's freedman, Polybius. He is short, and bearded, and so confident of his power and his talents that he seems bigger than other men. She hands him a scroll and he reads her writing aloud.

'*I hate him. I hate him. Oh it eats me.*'

On he reads, stopping to laugh and wink at her.

'*So close. To wrecking Tiberius...*'

'Oh well done, my little spider,' he says. 'Well done. There is power in your silence, do you see? Men want to fill in the gaps.'

She grins back. Holds out her hand for payment. The coins chink into her palm.

'Off you go, my free little spider,' he says. 'I will send for you again soon.'

He walks off, clutching her words in his small palm, his jaunty whistle echoing through the empty corridors.

Interview with Antonia Senior

Can you tell us a bit about yourself? How long have you been writing and what other jobs have you had?

My first job was on the insanely glamorous Pensions World magazine. I then became a personal finance journalist at The Times. I was on staff at the paper for years, and had a variety of jobs including Deputy Business Editor, Leader Writer, and Editor of the science magazine, Eureka. I left after my second child to concentrated on writing. I've written three published novels, and a couple more unpublished. I write a monthly column for the book section, rounding up the best new historical fiction releases.

What is it about Rome that inspires you?

I've always adored ancient history. I love the poetry, the philosophy, the battles, the personalities. It is a fantastic source of inspiration for stories, because it is at once alien and familiar. I love the City of Rome more than anywhere else on the planet. My most perfect day so far this year involved wondering about the Palatine, which was covered in wildflowers, followed by a long boozy lunch in a Roman trattoria. Then wondering though Renaissance Rome eating ice cream. Genuine heaven.

What inspired you to write this particular story?

This particular story came about when I read Ovid's poems from exile. They were so utterly despairing and human. He conjures such a vivid sense of being an exile, of the drabness and misery of his frontier life compared to the glory of Rome.

What do you enjoy most about writing?

Being transported to other worlds. Not having a boss.

If you were transported back to the time your story is set, who is the first person you would want to talk to and why?

I'd love to meet Seneca. He is such a fascinating mass of contradictions: a wealthy man who preaches moderation. A counsellor to a tyrant who talks so eloquently of the importance of freedom. A Stoic who could write stunning essays about controlling emotion and also tragedies which were consumed with passions. I would absolutely love to share a couch with him.

What would you bring back from ancient Rome with you?

Garum. I once made some for my daughter's Roman day at school and it was horrible. And it got dropped on the floor, and the classroom carpet smelled of anchovies for a month. Also books: Tiberius, Claudius, Agrippina – they all wrote their own accounts of their lives. Imagine if we had copies!

If there was one event in the period you could witness (in perfect safety) what would it be?

I would eavesdrop on the conversation between Augustus and his daughter Julia when he exiled her for life. One of the things that is so fascinating about Julio-Claudian Rome is the fact that all the politics were played out through these epic, familial dramas.

Why do you think readers are still so thirsty for stories from this period?

Rome has everything you need in a period to catch readers' attention. There are wars and tyrants, lovers and enemies. We all know a little bit about Rome, but there's always more to discover, always more stories to unearth.

How important is it for you to be part of a community of writers, and why?

It's vital to know other writers. Otherwise you have to drink alone.

Where can readers find out more about your books?

You can find out more about me at antoniasenior.com or follow me on Twitter @tonisenior

The Roman – Peter Tonkin

A *Caesar's Spies* story

i

'Roman Liburnian!' called the lookout.

Captain Barzan of the Cilician pirate trireme *Thalassa* looked up, saw the direction of the pointing arm and the sleek Roman vessel it was indicating. He turned to the helmsman, 'Come two points south. We can catch him before he reaches port.' He raised his voice, bellowing. 'Rowing master, standard speed, we'll let the oars assist the sail and perhaps overcome the drag from the weed on *Thalassa*'s bottom. Slave master, the men may sing the rowing song.'

The whole conversation had been audible below and the slave named 44 began easing his oar out before the *pausator* rowing-master started to pound the rhythm on his drum and the *hortator* slave-master began to sing the rowing song,

'*HEIA, Viri, nostruim reboans echo sonnet HEIA!*'

44 leaned forward swinging his oar into position, dropped the blade in concert with the other galley slaves and pulled with all his strength. To an experienced seafarer such as Captain Barzan, 44's name carried as much information as a patrician Roman name establishing identity through a paternal forename, family name and third name based on something personal. The name 44 revealed that the slave was a *thranite* a galley-slave who sat on the uppermost of *Thalassa*'s three levels of rowing benches in a box that reached out from the ship's side like a balcony on a building. That he was strong enough to control an oar in excess of twelve feet long. That he sat half way along the right side of the ship facing the stern. As 44 was one of the sixty two men who handled the most unwieldy oars, he needed the clearest view of the *pausator* and the *hortator* whose drum-beat and rowing song controlled rhythm and speed – until the ship went into battle and the singing had to stop.

More than a year at the oar broadened 44's shoulders and corded his arms; his back was as strong as his massive thighs. Even though he was young his palms were as calloused as anyone's aboard. As, indeed, were his naked buttocks and the soles of his feet. Together with the other oarsmen, he could power *Thalassa* across the sea at ten knots, even when the bottom was fouled, as now, with barnacles, mussels and weed.

*

The Liburnian's captain saw them coming and swung southward, racing towards the port of Rhodes. He was making almost seven knots under sail, but the wind was falling light. If he was going to get safely past the ruin of the Colossus, he was soon going to have to turn a few more points southwards and rely on his two banks of eighteen oars per side. Once that happened he would find himself utterly at the mercy of *Thalassa*'s three banks totalling eighty five a side, weed or no weed.

Captain Barzan looked down onto the main deck where his fifty-man crew waited, the deck-rail lined with pirates carrying grappling hooks. He glanced up once again, focusing all his attention on the Roman vessel that was his prey. It would be over in half an hour or so. Barzan, *Thalassa* and her crew would be richer by the worth of another hull and by whatever or whoever they found aboard worth selling at auction, in the slave markets of Delos or holding for ransom.

'*There!*' called the lookout once again. The Roman captain had turned one point too far away from the wind and it had deserted him. His empty sail flapped like a broken wing. The Liburnian's sleek hull wallowed. Her oars came out and began to beat the surface in a vain attempt at escape. Too little, thought Barzan, and far too late. 'Battle speed!' he bellowed and the singing on the rowing decks stopped.

ii

Half an hour later 44 sat with his oar on his lap, cold and dripping; the moisture from the shaft mixed with the perspiration running down his lower belly and the inside of his thighs. His seat in the upper and outer position meant that he overhung the Liburnian's deck slightly. If he angled the oar-blade, he could see what was going on. The pirates jumped down scant feet away and he watched them go to work. The Liburnian's crew were merchantmen not soldiers. Given the chance they would have surrendered before Captain Barzan's men came aboard but they didn't get the opportunity. Those who stood against the pirates were ruthlessly chopped down. The rest were herded across the red-running deck towards the forecastle, freeing the stern for the last of those who still wanted to fight: the captain, a couple of his senior officers and a young Roman passenger. He was in armour and laying about himself with a *gladius* but he lacked both helmet and shield. He probably had slaves and body servants below but he really needed a couple of stout legionaries to back him up.

It was brave, but 44 could see that the odds were far beyond anything the Roman could match. Would he elect ignominious life or glorious death? 44 knew which one he would have chosen. Footsteps thumped across the deck above 44's head; the rail creaked as a sizeable body leaned against it. 'Well?' bellowed Barzan. 'Make your minds up. Wind's shifting, tide's turning and I haven't got all day.'

The Liburnian's captain and senior officers threw their weapons down. Only the Roman stood firm, his eyes narrowed in calculation. The hulls groaned against each-other as a wave ran under them heading for Rhodes. The ropes attached to the grappling hooks hummed like lyre-strings. 'Ransom Roman,' offered Barzan. 'We'll keep you safe, feed you and water you at our own expense if you give us your word. You look as though you'd be worth a *sestercius* or two.'

The Roman still hesitated. One of the pirates stepped silently in behind him and hit him on the head with the pommel of his sword. The Roman crashed to the deck and his *gladius* spun away. 'Good decision,' said Barzan to the unconscious man. 'Bring him aboard and let's get going.'

*

44 was only able to hear what happened later that day after the Liburnian's crew had been secured below and replaced by pirates so that she could follow in *Thalassa*'s wake. But he had seen it all before.

'You can't treat me like this!' snarled the prisoner's scholarly Greek. 'I am a Roman citizen!'

'OH!' gasped Barzan, '*A Roman citizen*! If only we had *known*... What are we poor Cilician pirates to do in the face of a citizen of the Republic?'

There was a brief silence. The game could go one of two ways now, thought 44. If the arrogant Roman took Barzan at his word he would be stripped, given sandals and a toga, shown to a ladder down the ship's side and sent on his way – for, as every Cilician pirate knew, there was nothing a Roman citizen could not do. Including walking on water.

But this Roman, it seemed, was no pompous fool with an over-inflated opinion of himself. 'You're mocking me!' he said. 'An entire ship-full of pirates cowed by one man – Roman citizen or not! You are simply laughing at me!'

'We are indeed,' answered Barzan cheerfully. 'Let's hope we do not also laugh at your ransom!' He paused. 'We were thinking twenty talents. Silver.'

'*Twenty talents*,' replied the Roman. 'Have you no idea who I am? I am worth at least twice that. Send to my friends in Miletus and they will supply forty talents at least. No! Fifty. *Silver*!'

'We'll be happy to do as you advise!' answered Barzan. 'Fifty talents it is!'

'But be warned,' continued the Roman. 'When the money is paid and my freedom is restored, I will return with a fleet. I will track you down, I will take back my silver. And I will crucify you all.'

After the laughter died down, 44 heard Barzan demand, 'By what name should we know our Nemesis?'

'I am Gaius, son of Gaius of the Julii family which owes its direct descent to the Goddess Venus Victrix. And, in honour of a distinguished ancestor famous for single-handedly killing an elephant, I am also known as Caesar.'

'So, young Gaius Julius Caesar, we have a bargain. You owe us fifty silver talents for your freedom...'

'And crucifixion for having interrupted my journey to Molon's school of oratory in Rhodes,' concluded the Roman grimly.

iii

'Let us consider, fellow senators, the damage that piracy does to the Republic,' said Gaius Julius Caesar. His voice, echoed across the anchorage. 'How many ways does this iniquitous pastime hurt Rome and her citizens? Obviously, to begin with, it is responsible for the damage to legitimate trade and the theft of Roman goods, leading to the ruin of Roman commercial enterprises. Furthermore...'

44 listened to Caesar's speech, inflicted on the pirates because he could not practice it with the famous elocution teacher Molon whose most notable recent pupil was Marcus Tullius Cicero. *Thalassa* sat at anchor in the makeshift harbour of Barzan's favourite inlet on the pirate island of Pharmacusa after the better part of a fortnight running north. She sat there alone, for the captured Liburnian, stripped of her officers and crew, had been sent to Miletus with the ransom demand. Teams of slaves dived beneath *Thalassa* to clean her hull while her crew repaired her upper works, masts and rigging. Barzan's success relied on the way he maintained his ship and treated his galley-slaves as well as upon the fierceness of his crew. Recent times, however, had been lean and hard. But now the promise of Caesar's ransom meant he had time and space to indulge in repairs and clean the foul hull while everyone took a well-earned rest. The galley slaves sat on the sand under lackadaisical guard.

The guards were apathetic because the day was hot and the slaves sluggish. In any case there was nowhere to run to on Pharmacusa except to other pirate captains in other bays – most of them far worse than Barzan. Or to the forested peaks of the island's hilly spine, compared with which the sea seemed more inviting. But few slaves, like few sailors, could swim and anyone risking the waters who didn't drown immediately would probably find themselves food for the sharks.

Except for the team cleaning *Thalassa*'s hull, most of the galley-slaves sat mindlessly, glad that they had been able to wash as they waded ashore and grateful that they were out of the ship as their rowing benches were sluiced and the bilges purified. But 44 was thinking of much more than current ease. He understood that the captive awaiting his ransom was different to anyone Barzan had held before. The crew might have been amused by the Roman's arrogant ways since the ransom demands had been sent out but 44 remembered the threat of crucifixion. And, while the others found the warning just another element in the Roman's amusing pomposity, 44 believed Caesar had every intention of carrying it out. Furthermore, he reckoned that when the Roman returned with his ships and his soldiers, a quick-thinking young galley-slave might grasp a chance at freedom.

44 allowed Caesar's Greek elocution to sweep over him, reminding him of his youth, even though it had an Athenian accent and 44 was a Spartan who had been brought up in the old ways which were little more than legends recounted to Roman tourists these days. He had strangled a wolf with his bare hands before he slept with his first woman. He was extremely adept at killing and had been captured by the slave traders who sold him to Barzan as he sought to finish the rituals of manhood and join a *kryptaeia* secret service unit by killing his first man. Although on the one hand he was still a helpless galley-slave, on the other he was a fully- fledged Spartan warrior who would have been perfectly capable of standing with Leonidas and his Three Hundred at the gates of Thermopylae.

'Shit,' said the *hortator*, staring out to where *Thalassa* sat on the silvery bay. 'That's another slave gone. It's just impossible to keep a close eye on them all.' 44 sat up and squinted. There was a body floating face-down beside hull.

'We'll never clean her keel at this rate,' said the *gubernator*. The two men shook their heads.

Another piece of 44's plan fell into place.

*

'Sails!' called the lookout late next morning. 'Two vessels hull-down on the horizon.'

'It has to be our Liburnian,' said Barzan. 'Coming back with the ransom and a ship to take our prisoner home.'

'It'd better be the ransom,' growled the *gubernator*. 'I wouldn't give an *obol* for Caesar's chances otherwise. One more speech and they'll tear him to pieces like the mad Maenads ripping Orpheus to shreds.'

'True enough,' agreed the *hortator*. 'He hasn't made any friends with all those endless fucking speeches. And as for the poems...'

Caesar's pirate audience stirred as the Liburnian and its companion approached. 'What!' he bellowed. 'I haven't finished my speech! Will you Cilician clods just sit and listen...' But the promise of so much money – after more than a month of listening to Caesar - was too much to be controlled.

The Liburnian docked first but her crew called that the silver was on the other vessel. The second ship was immediately invaded by excited pirates. Sure enough it carried fifty silver talents, each weighing about the same as a man, which were carried onto the rudimentary dockside by the triumphant pirates. Caesar finally gave up on his speeches and shouldered his way up the gangplank greeting and being greeted by the men who had come to free him.

As soon as the weighty talents had been unloaded and checked, Caesar returned to the head of the gangway. 'After thirty-eight days of my captivity, things are finally settled between us,' he called down to Barzan. 'My slaves and body-servants have packed away everything I brought with me. They will now bring my possessions aboard so that I can leave you and return to Miletus. But remember what I promised. I will be back!'

He departed Pharmacusa to hoots of derisive merriment. Even the slaves laughed.

Except for 44.

iv

'That bloody Roman may have handed us a poisoned chalice,' said Barzan to the *gubernator*, his oldest friend and most trusted companion. 'This amount of silver on an island full of pirates is likely to draw unwelcome attention.'

'What can we do?'

'We can't keep it here and guard it ourselves, especially as I want to set sail again as soon as possible. Nor can we keep it aboard *Thalassa*. Everyone would be more worried about losing this treasure than about getting even more. We had better hide it.'

'On the island?'

'Up in the hills. I've been planning this ever since that arrogant Roman offered an unmanageable fortune as his ransom. I wouldn't be surprised if he hoped we'd kill each-other as we all tried to get it for ourselves!'

'No, Captain, that can't be true – he's going to come back and *crucify* us; that's his real plan!'

The two men had a good laugh at that.

44 did not share their amusement. It was not hard to eavesdrop on them as long as his actions weren't too obvious. He was only a galley-slave after all – a thing of no account, so easy to overlook.

'You'll need two men per talent to carry it, though – that's nearly half the oarsmen,' said the *gubernator* when their hilarity died down.

'We'll put it all aboard the Liburnian for the time-being. Tie her up by the dockside so no-one has to carry anything too far. Set a well-armed guard. Then we can do it over the next few days as we get *Thalassa* re-rigged, clean and ready to sail. Ten men. Five talents a time. Ten visits to my hiding place. Problem solved.'

'Ten men? Why so few?'

'I trust *myself* not to give the location away. And I trust *you*. But I can't trust anyone else. So we'll choose the ten worst oarsmen. Ones we won't miss when we set sail again. They'll take the talents up and we'll isolate them each time they come back – but they won't be coming back from the last excursion at all. Besides, the work on *Thalassa*'s hull is progressing more slowly than I calculated. We have time to do it little by little.'

*

'I can swim,' called 44. 'I'll go and work on the hull. Better than sitting here day after day getting eaten alive by sand-flies...'

The slave-master hesitated. 44 was his best oarsman - too good to risk. But then again, it was well over a week since Caesar left and time was running out along with Barzan's patience. The last of the talents was due to be moved tomorrow, the captain wanted to leave as soon as possible after that and *Thalassa* was not yet clean.

44 waded into the water and leaned forward when it reached his waist, swimming out to *Thalassa* with powerful strokes. He pulled himself up the nearest ladder and a crewman handed him a chisel and a hammer. 'I'll need these back,' he warned. 'The captain wants a careful count kept.'

44 nodded, took a deep breath and dived beneath the trireme's keel. Several other figures were at work, their bodies blurred by the water. There were three teams. One armed like him with hammer and chisel attacking the barnacles encrusting the hull. Another with short knives cutting the strings of mussels free and scraping the remnants the chisels left. And a third with long, sharp knives whose job was to hack the weed free so the others could get at the mussels and barnacles. Timing it so that he moved only when he was unobserved, 44 left his job and began to search the sea-bed below the ship. The last slave floating face-down would have been too busy drowning to give his equipment back. But there was nothing he could use as a weapon there – the crew were clearly being very careful indeed. He was called in at day's end and given extra food with the rest of the surviving divers.

He was back in the freezing water soon after dawn and once again he had no trouble leaving the others unobserved. It took him one lung-bursting breath to swim underwater to the shelter of the dock. He hid there until he heard Barzan bring the ten slaves to retrieve the last five talents, then he slid out of the water and began to exercise some of the skills he had learned as he grew up. Using the bushes for cover, 44 followed them up into the hillside forest. Unarmed, naked and thankful for the gathering heat of the morning, he flitted through the forest, haunting the laden sailors' footsteps like a *fantasma*.

In the past, it had taken the oarsmen most of the daylight hours to carry the silver away, conceal it and return. But it didn't take that long to discover where the treasure was hidden. 44 watched them as they began to conceal the last five talents then he returned to the dockside, slid back into the water and went to work under *Thalassa* having been absent for three hours, his jaunt unnoticed by the bored and listless guards on shore or aboard.

Barzan returned alone mid-afternoon. By evening the cleaning of *Thalassa*'s hull was complete. 44 was among the team that pulled the trireme to the jetty and secured her beside the Liburnian. 'Right,' announced Barzan. 'Both crews and slaves eat and rest tonight. Board *Thalassa* and our new Liburnian at first light tomorrow and we will be out on the hunt by sunrise.'

44 was awake with the first of *Thalassa*'s crew as the sky began to lighten. Under the direction of the *pausator* and the *hortator* they found their places, sat on the familiar benches and slid the oars out. Barzan himself came aboard last. 'Right!' he bellowed, his voice carrying to the Liburnian. 'Lets go!' The oarsmen eased the vessels out into deeper water, then swung *Thalassa* round so that she was heading for the opening of the bay.

But no sooner had the *pausator* set the rhythm than the captain called, 'All stop!'

The slaves sat still and silent, wondering what was going on. They didn't have to wait long to find out. One of the sailors leaned down, one hand on the *pausator*'s drum. 'There's a fleet of Roman triremes blockading the bay!'

'It's that bastard we ransomed,' growled the *pausator*. 'Come back to crucify us all. Just like he said he would!'

44 found himself nodding in agreement, scarcely able to control his excitement.

'What shall we do, Captain?' The *gubernator*'s question was just audible.

'Let me think!' snarled Barzan.

Fight! Thought 44. Fight and die with honour! But he knew very well that Barzan would never do that. He had too many friends amongst the crews. He loved *Thalassa* and would never see her or the Liburnian rammed, fired or falling back into Roman hands. He even had some kindness for 44 and his companions. No. Even before Barzan realised the inevitable, 44 knew that he would try and bargain with the Roman who had become their nemesis after all.

v

'If you release us, I will return the ransom,' offered Barzan.

'You are a mere pirate,' came Caesar's icy answer. 'So I can hardly expect you to understand the concept of honour. But when a man of the Julii gives his word, he keeps it no matter what the danger or the cost. I said I would return: I have. I said I would bring a fleet: I have. I said I would crucify you and your crew. I will. Whether the ransom is returned or not.'

Some whim of Caesar's made him hold the negotiations with Barzan on the dockside in front of the Cilician captain's condemned crew and the two sets of galley-slaves who had powered *Thalassa* and the Liburnian – whose fate was yet to be decided. Though 44 suspected they were all bound for the slave markets at Delos – especially if Barzan went to Hades without revealing where the ransom was hidden. Marines from the fleet blockading the bay formed a wall of steel around the captives. The morning was ominously still, the sky a steely blue; away in the west there was a wall of black thunderheads: bad weather on the way.

'Very well, then,' spat Barzan with the courage of a cornered rat. 'If we die anyway then you can whistle for your fifty talents!'

'I could torture the information out of you,' Caesar pointed out. 'I have *carnifexes* adept in the use of whips, hooks, hammers and hot irons.'

'Would that be *honourable*, Caesar? You promised crucifixion. There was no talk of butchers or branding irons.'

'Very well,' said Caesar. 'Let it be so.'

The fleet's carpenters made short work of preparing fifty crosses. Long before the black clouds were overhead they were laid out on the dockside. Barzan and his crew were lashed in place while the galley slaves dug pits deep enough for the crosses to stand in once they were pulled erect. The carpenters returned with long nails and heavy hammers.

44 had joined the team digging the hole for Barzan's cross. He knew Caesar would take a personal interest in the captain's execution. The carpenter rested his first nail on the pale flesh of Barzan's right wrist beside the rope that held it immovably in place. He raised the hammer ready to drive it through and into the wood beneath. Caesar appeared. 'Take special care,' he said. 'There are vessels in the wrist that allow a swift and easy death if they are cut. I do not want them cut. Death must not come too easily for this one.'

'As you say, *dominus*.' The carpenter drove the nail down between the veins and arteries in the pirate's right wrist, through the tendons, bones and skin, deep into the wood. Then he did the same to the left wrist. Barzan grunted and groaned but he did not cry out until the nails smashed through his ankles.

*

Some time later, Barzan and his crew were hanging, their shattered ankles perhaps two Roman feet above the ground. Their bodies pulled forward by the weight of their heads, shoulders and bellies, their arms reaching back like the wings of birds about to take flight, chests fully expanded by the position, breathing almost impossible. Even so, Barzan fought to have the last word. 'Look at us, Gaius Julius Caesar! Your stupid Roman arrogance may have cost us our lives but it has cost you fifty talents. The weight of each man hanging here. *In silver*!'

44 stepped forward, his movement just enough to catch the Roman's eye without disturbing the guards. '*Kyrios*, Lord,' he said quietly. 'I know where your silver is.'

Caesar turned. He saw a tall, broad-shouldered young man – perhaps five years his junior. His unkempt hair curled into ringlets of red gold. The beard beginning to cover his chin shone with copper highlights, as did the hair matted on his chest, belly and groin. His face was not delicate – strong rather than beautiful but striking nevertheless. His eyes were dark brown with the strangest reddish tint. Caesar was by no means proof against male beauty. So he was willing to indulge the interruption.

'You know where the ransom is hidden?'

'I followed them as they hid it, *kyrios*.'

Barzan came to his galley-slave's aid – by accident rather than design. 'You treacherous bastard,' he spat, heaving his body into agonising positions so he could catch sufficient breath to speak. 'I should have made you one of the slaves who carried the treasure and slit your throat at the end!'

'Just so,' said Caesar with a cold glance at the snarling man. He looked back at 44 as the captain choked back into silence, almost suffocated by what he had managed to say. 'And what do you want in return for showing me where the treasure is?'

'My freedom. I know you will send the others to the slave markets on Delos. Give me my freedom.'

'Your freedom? That's *all*? For the weight of fifty men in silver? No reward? No weapons? No clothes? No way off the island?'

'I can find all these for myself, Caesar. Once I am free. All I need is your word. The word of a man of the Julii.'

'Very well, you have my word. What will you need to retrieve the fifty talents? Carts?'

'No, *kyrios*. It is hidden where only men on foot may go.'

'Men then. Will a hundred be enough?'

'Yes, *kyrios*.'

'You have them. But slave, you also have my word on this: if you are trying to trick me, if this is a ruse to allow you to escape and my silver is not returned, then I will hunt you as I have hunted these pirates and when I catch you, you will beg for an easy death like your captain and his men are enjoying.'

'I am telling the truth, *kyrios*. I will lead your men to the hiding place and we will return with your silver.'

Caesar nodded and as he did so, the first great flash of lightning came with an immediate clap of thunder as though a volcano was exploding into life nearby.

Afterward

'He was a good captain,' said 44, looking up at Barzan's rain-drenched corpse hanging on the cross. 'He treated us slaves well enough.' The thunderstorm was pulling away but the last of the rain pounded down onto the men loading Caesar's silver aboard *Thalassa*, which was secured beside the Liburnian at the dockside and which was also the Roman's property now, along with the slaves who rowed her. All except for one of them.

'Your fellow slaves tell me you are known as 44,' said Caesar. 'And sometimes *Spartacus* – the Spartan. These are not good names for a free man; I could not write either on your manumission papers. What name were you known by before you were taken and enslaved? What name did your father give you at your birth?'

'I never knew my father or the name he gave me. I was found on a hillside in Sparta as a baby and taken in by shepherds. They called me The Gift of Artemis, because she is the goddess of childbirth and wild places. They called me Artemidorus.'

'You have much to learn, young Artemidorus,' said Caesar as he signed the papers freeing 44 from slavery. 'You should not judge men solely by their actions. You also need to understand their motivations. The captain treated you slaves well, but only because he needed you fit enough to power his vessel. Had he needed you to die, you would be dead like the men who carried his silver; like the men who drowned careening his ship.'

The Roman's gaze grew distant, as though he was considering something far away in distance or time. 'Consider, if a man is standing behind you with a dagger in his hand, it is his motivation that is important. If he is motivated to kill you, then his actions are hardly relevant, all except that one. No matter how friendly he might seem to your face; no matter how sympathetic or sycophantic - his motivation is all important. Every time he does not stab you in the back is merely one step nearer to the moment when he *will* stab you in the back. Do you understand?'

'Yes *kyrios*, I understand,' said Artemidorus as he took his manumission papers. 'You should never let anyone carrying a dagger come too close to your back.'

Interview with Peter Tonkin

Can you tell us about yourself?

I was born in Co Londonderry, January 1950. My father was an RAF officer so I was raised not only in Ireland but in RAF camps all over England, Europe and the Middle East. At school I acted and sang as well as writing poetry and short stories. English was my favorite subject (closely followed by history – my favorite text was *Julius Caesar* where my Roman stories all began).

When I went to University (Queen's Belfast) I continued to act and write poetry – which was fortunate as after a 'Fresher' year studying English, Philosophy and History (with renowned medievalist Professor Rev. Dr W L Warren) I was accepted into the honours school of English where my professors included Seamus Heaney, Edna Longley and Alexander McCall Smith while my fellow students included Paul Muldoon, Bernard MacLaverty and Ciaran Hinds who played Hamlet in my production of the Bad Quarto, and – much later – Caesar in the famous HBO series *Rome*.

How long have you been writing and what other jobs have you had?

I left Queen's in 1975 and became a teacher in London. I continued to write. My first international bestseller, *Killer* was published in 1978. Two years later I married and by 1990 had started a family. My wife Charmaine and I have two sons, Guy and Mark. During my 30 year career, rising to the positions of Assistant Headteacher and Examiner in A Level Law, I completed the 30-volume *Mariner* series of action adventures.

On retiring, I widened my horizons adding the *Master of Defence* series of Elizabethan murder-mysteries as well as the *Caesar's Spies* series of Roman spy stories, both closely based on real historical characters and events.

What is it about Rome that inspired you?

I studied Latin at school and the resultant fascination with Ancient Rome was underpinned by my love of history, all of which came together when I began work on *The Ides*, a reconstruction of the day Caesar died from the point of view of Artemidorus, a real historical figure who handed Caesar a list naming the men planning to kill him. Caesar never read it and it was found on his corpse. I imagined Artemidorus as a soldier working undercover for Antony with orders to protect Caesar.

Can you tell us about other work inspired by Rome?

Despite failing in that assignment, Artemidorus has now continued to serve Antony through three more novels which recreate the actual historical events after Caesar's death. (*After the Ides, Cicero Dies* and *The Road To War*) The next one, *Philippi*, is fully prepared – but on hold while I am finishing *A Verse To Murder*, number six in the *Master of Defence* series; novel number 43 overall.

Rome as a historical subject and as a city has fascinated me all my life. Charmaine and I go there at least once a year (and, as Cleopatra plays an important part in the Roman series, we also regularly visit Egypt). Since retiring, we are free to travel and follow Hammond Innes' famous advice – if you are writing about a place, go there. So Hadrian's Wall, Chester, Bath, Stratford, a range of sites in London as well as Rome, Egypt and the Mediterranean coast from Gibraltar to Italy all get regular visits.

What inspired you to write this particular story?

The Roman, is one of a proposed triptych describing Artemidorus' youth, time as a galley slave and eventual meeting with Caesar which never actually got written. The project of putting together *Rubicon* focused my mind and I was keen to work on it despite the fact that I was part-way through an Elizabethan novel. As most of this collection's readership will know, this too is based on one of the most famous of the young Caesar's exploits.

What do you enjoy most about writing?

I love the freedom writing gives to explore characters, times and situations that would otherwise remain closed or remote. I metaphorically rub shoulders with figures such as Caesar, Antony and Cleopatra. I have met them in other books – both factual and fictional - but writing about them allows me to get to know them personally (whether that knowledge is historically accurate or not).

If you were transported back to the time your story is set, who would be the first person you would want to talk to and why?

Were I to return to those times, I would be standing beside Artemidorus on 15 March 710 AUC urging Caesar to think twice before trusting Brutus, Cassius and the rest.

What would you bring back from Ancient Rome with you?

Were I as unsuccessful as Artemidorus in that endeavor I would want to bring back Brutus' dagger, which delivered the last – though not the fatal – blow, and which he immortalized with Cassius' on the obverse of the coins they struck to pay their armies in the east.

Why do you think readers are still so thirsty for stories from this period?

The fascination with the period seems endless. I first read *Ben-Hur* as a child and I have it on my Kindle now (where almost all of my own books are also readily available). I have an autographed photograph of Charlton Heston in the chariot race from the 1956 film version (still the greatest of all epics) on my study wall. It seems I am by no means alone in finding such stories, their settings, characters and epic qualities eternally fascinating.

How important is it for you to be part of a community of writers and why?

The community of writers brought together by the internet is vast. Historical writers seem to be even more approachable, enthusiastic and willing to share ideas than anyone else. It is a community I am proud to belong to and I plan to remain a part of it for a long time to come as Artemidorus and I become entangled in the events between Philippi and Actium – and then, briefly, tragically, beyond.

The Wedding - L.J. Trafford

I.

It was never easy to hold the emperor's attention. He was prone to distraction, whether it be the latest chariot racing results or a sudden inspiration for a poem. Either of which could grip hold of him for hours, whilst the unsigned scrolls lay forgotten on a desk.

Not this time though. Epaphroditus, Private Secretary to his Imperial Majesty Nero Caesar, had planned his moment perfectly. The races had concluded the previous afternoon, giving Nero a clear twelve hours to lament the result. Dire punishments had been cursed upon both the captain of the Blues, for daring to win, and the captain of the Greens, for such a miserably awful performance.

Sated by imaging violent deaths for all concerned (including the spectators who had cheered the winning Blues over the finish line) Nero was then presented with a visiting Greek poet. Several hours of culture later, the poet had managed to extract from the emperor an epic verse that had the Blue team obliterated by one of Jupiter's thunderbolts. The final line, concerning the smell of singed horse flesh, had Epaphroditus' innards wincing at its sheer awfulness. But it at least conveyed the obsessive passion for the races that afflicted the emperor.

Artistic needs met, Nero's more bodily wants were dealt with by a serving of light dishes. The secretary needed Nero full enough to not be distracted by hunger, but not so full as to nod off during Epaphroditus' reading of the latest report from the Northern Provinces. Or as Nero referred to them: The savage lands of barbarians.

The secretary hoped to avoid yet another discussion on why Rome bothered with them when they didn't even have theatres or art or poetry! Usually a list of the gold, silver and pearls, which the Northern Empire possessed in abundance, was enough to forestall a sudden Imperial declaration that Rome should just forget about those hairy barbarians and concentrate on the civilised world. Usually.

Today Epaphroditus had high hopes he would get to the end of the report without interruption. Nero was reclining on a couch sipping at a glass of asparagus juice (good for his voice, so the Greek poet had claimed) and the gaze from those watery blue eyes was friendly. The emperor appeared relaxed, happy even. This was the perfect moment.

"Imperial Majesty," said Epaphroditus, stepping forward with his head bowed respectfully.

"Ahhh, Epaphroditus," replied Nero. "What do you have for me today?"

"Imperial Majesty, I bring the provincial reports."

Beside Epaphroditus stood his assistant, Philo (possessed of the fastest shorthand in the palace), whose role today was to hand the scroll to his boss. This he did with his customary efficiency at the exact moment the secretary concluded his speech.

Epaphroditus cleared his throat and read, "Germania Inferior deliver their best wishes for the_."

The best wishes of those inferior Germans were cut short by a yawn. A yawn the likes of which had never been naturally produced. It was exaggerated to the extreme, loud and long, and geared solely to attract attention. It came not from the emperor, but rather from the creature who reclined beside him. It was dressed in a blue gown sewn with pearls that might well have come from the Northern Provinces, and a matching pearl studded tiara pinned to ringletted red hair. A hand with long perfectly manicured nails was pressed over its painted lips, failing to disguise the noise.

Epaphroditus ignored it. "Germania Inferior_"

Y.A.W.N.

Epaphroditus shot it a look. It smiled back at him, and then winked.

"Poppaea, my dear," fussed Nero, brushing his hand over its bare arm. "Are you well, my love?"

A bottom lip trembled a little, causing Nero to enquire, "What is it, my love? What ails you?" He held onto its hands, his eyes now full of concern.

"Oh my love," it said, before executing a fake swoon backwards, complete with sweeping arm.

"Oh Poppaea, Poppaea!" cried Nero. "My Poppaea is fatigued! Slaves! Quickly! We must take her to the Imperial bedchamber."

Epaphroditus stood back as four burly slaves rushed forward. They lifted the creature, who wasn't so fatigued that it couldn't snap at them not to crease its gown, and transported it to the door. The emperor rushed in front of them, crying, "I'll clear the way! We must hurry! Hurry!"

Looking over the shoulder of a slave, the creature made sure it gave the secretary a farewell wave before it was carried away.

Epaphroditus held it together for a count of twenty after their departure, before flinging the scroll across the room. It hit the wall with a disappointing 'pfft'. Philo ran over to retrieve it.

"That is it!" stormed Epaphroditus, as Philo tried to manipulate out the bent he'd caused on the Northern provinces report. "It goes. That thing goes!"

"Sir?" enquired Philo, handing him back the battered scroll.

"That thing. That thing playing Poppaea. That damned eunuch!"

"Sporus, sir?"

"Yes, Sporus!" fumed Epaphroditus. "How many other eunuchs do we have in the palace pretending to be the dead empress?"

It was obviously rhetorical, but Philo was made from very literally minded material. "Only Sporus, sir. So far." Then added, "He is very good at it, sir."

"Oh I know he is. He is far too good at it. That's the problem." Epaphroditus sat down on the emperor's deserted couch. "I accepted it at first. It seemed to be aiding the emperor in his grief over the empress' unfortunate death."

Which was how Poppaea's demise at the hands of her husband was spoken of in the palace; 'unfortunate'. An 'unfortunate' accident that had Nero's foot colliding with Poppaea's pregnant stomach, killing both mother and potential heir.

"But now? It's been months and the emperor shows no sign of dropping his fantasy that Poppaea is still alive. Of course it doesn't help that the damned eunuch can impersonate the empress to her very gesture. Nor that it seems quite happy to pretend to be someone else. I have a bad feeling about which way this thing is headed. Before we know it Sporus will be insisting upon accompanying the emperor to the Senate House, overseeing the Bona Dea festival and having dinner with the Chief Vestal!"

He winced at the very plausibility of it. Nobody wanted to be the one to break down Nero's delusion. Certainly not Epaphroditus. He valued his life far too much. Something Sporus was taking full advantage of.

"It's also not helping the financial situation, sir," interjected Philo.

Epaphroditus looked up. "How so?"

It took Philo's prodigious memory quite some time to reel off the entire list of Sporus' expenditure as empress, particularly as he'd organised the spending into helpful subheadings such as: bronze headwear, silver plated headwear, gold plated headwear, headwear containing additional jewels and so forth.

By the end of this catalogue of waste (in Epaphroditus' view – for Sporus was now in possession of enough dresses to change twice a day for the next year) the secretary had made a decision.

"That eunuch goes."

A statement Philo felt compelled to record in the note tablet he was never without. After scrawling this in the wax, he asked anxiously. "Sir?"

"The emperor will remarry," said Epaphroditus. "He simply cannot keep up this farce when there is a new empress on his arm. One that is an actual woman!"

***

ii.

Calvia Crispinilla, Nero's Mistress of the Wardrobe, palace party planner extraordinaire and dresser of that damned eunuch, strode into Epaphroditus' office. She was accompanied by a flurry of slave girls present to cater to her every whim, and Philo, whom she'd had a whim the slave girls should push out of her way when he asked her politely her business with Epaphroditus.

"I'm sorry, sir," began Philo, hurrying ahead of Calvia. "I know you don't like to be interrupted unannounced, sir."

"Quite," said Calvia, sitting herself down. "Who knows what depraved act you might walk in on."

"The Treasury report," said Epaphroditus, using a stylus to point at the scroll unrolled in front of him.

"Filthy stuff, I'm sure. I have important news." She leaned forward. "I have found the most astounding tunic for the emperor's wedding. Truly. It is astonishing. It has to be seen to be believed. It's magnificent."

"And the bride?" asked Epaphroditus. "Have you found an astounding one of those yet?"

Calvia waved her hand. "That's all sorted. Now, I want to talk about the arrangements. I'm thinking the grand banqueting hall for the day time events_"

"You found an empress?" interrupted Epaphroditus. "For the emperor?"

Calvia, adjusted the shawl draped across her shoulders, "I said I would, did I not? And I did. Lovely girl. Perfect."

"And she is?" prompted the secretary. Beside him Philo whipped out a note tablet ready.

"Statilia Messalina."

As a grand announcement it fell somewhat short.

"Never heard of her," said Epaphroditus.

"Which is one of many reasons why she is perfect. Statilia Messalina is of a good, suitably noble family bursting to the brim with Senators and others of that ilk. She's been married three times. Which is a good thing," she stressed, before Epaphroditus could interrupt her. "Because it means she'll not be shocked by some of the emperor's more 'specialist' requirements."

"Age?"

"Early 30's. Young enough to beget an heir for his Imperial Majesty but old enough to appeal to the emperor's preference for the more mature lady."

Epaphroditus sat back in his chair. "She sounds suitable."

"You said, find a suitable bride. I did. She's also very pretty."

"Good."

"But," added Calvia, rising to her feet. "If you think any of that will dislodge Sporus I fear you will be disappointed."

"It will," insisted Epaphroditus. "It most definitely will."

***

The wedding of Nero Claudius Germanicus Drusus to Statilia Messalina occurred five days later. Such was the speed of the arrangements that popular palace gossip claimed Statilia herself only found out about the wedding when she arrived for a dinner invitation and was handed the brides' scarlet veil. To Epaphroditus' mind it was just in time. That damned eunuch had started to complain of nausea and the secretary harboured a horrible suspicion that it was about to announce a pregnancy.

Epaphroditus straightened his wedding outfit. In celebration he'd upped his usual muted style to a green tunic hemmed with gold braiding. It should be one terrific party. Epaphroditus had seen the list of events Calvia had organised and even he, jaded palace party goer that he was, was inwardly bouncing with anticipation. Utterly unlike his fellow wedding attendee, Philo, who stood in the doorway in his standard white palace issued tunic, looking thoroughly miserable.

Aware of his assistant's great dislike of unstructured gatherings for the purposes of fun, Epaphroditus said, "You'll enjoy it." Philo looked unconvinced. "It's the party of the year! Perhaps even the decade!"

Philo fiddled with the strap on his satchel, avoiding his boss' gaze.

"Obviously I'll expect a full report on it."

Philo looked up, his expression quizzical.

"Somebody needs to record the full detail of the event," he continued. "So that we may fully study what parts were successful and which parts were less successful. Your findings can be used to inform future weddings. Not that we'll have any in the near future. This one is set to last." So Epaphroditus had decided.

"I think that could be useful, sir," said Philo, after a moment's consideration.

"I think so too," said the secretary, hoping that Philo would at least relax enough to enjoy a little of the day's festivities. He clapped his palms together. "Right! We'd better go see this thing through."

A declaration immediately thwarted by the simultaneous arrival of two Imperial messengers.

"Sir, the emperor demands your presence. He wishes to cancel the wedding."

Of course he did.

"Sir, the eunuch's on the loose."

Of course it was.

Used to crisis management, Imperial service was nothing but one long crisis, Epaphroditus responded calmly.

"Philo, you handle the Sporus situation. I'll deal with the emperor."

***

Epaphroditus found the emperor standing in the centre of his chamber in what was, as Calvia had promised, a truly astonishing wedding tunic. It was sunshine yellow in a shade that had the secretary squinting at its brightness. The rest of the outfit consisted of a red cape and spiky diadem crusted with rubies. Epaphroditus recognised Calvia's vision: Nero was to be Apollo, the sun God. His yellow beam to join with his bride's fiery scarlet veil.

It was a shame that the Emperor was not radiating this vision; Epaphroditus doubted Apollo was given to such mopes.

"Oh Epaphroditus!" whined the emperor, kicking away the two slaves who fussed at his cape alignment. "What about Poppaea?"

"Imperial Majesty," began Epaphroditus, in the soft tone he often used to placate his children. "Did we not discuss this yesterday?"

Nero brushed his hands through the air. "I know, I know! But Poppaea! I don't see_"

"As we discussed Caesar, Poppaea agrees to this marriage because she recognises the importance of an heir for Caesar. She has been most insistent on that point and I have to say, very dignified. It becomes her majesty that she has chosen to step aside for the good of her husband and the Empire."

"She might yet have a child_" pouted Nero.

Epaphroditus held his hands apart, showing his palms. "Alas, the doctors are all in agreement, Caesar. But as we discussed this does not mean that Caesar may not visit Poppaea occasionally if he desires."

Nero's head bobbed up and down, the diadem bouncing on his curls.

"It is necessary though for Caesar to marry and produce an heir. It is his duty."

"Duty!" cried Nero, his eyes moistening. "Should the Gods punish me so! To make me divorce the woman I adore with all my heart!"

"It is as Poppaea wishes, Caesar."

"Such a good woman, such a wonderful woman. To sacrifice herself for me! I do not deserve her. But I shall do her will, Epaphroditus, I shall!" The pout stiffened in resolve.

"Statilia Messalina is an exceptionally beautiful woman," slipped in the secretary.

"Naturally," said Nero." I would not marry less. I am emperor."

***

iii.

Since the marriage announcement Sporus had fallen into a weeping, wailing grief. At first there had been sympathy for the heartbroken eunuch. A whole army of slave girls had sat up late into the night listening to his woes, offering a soft bosom for him to lean on and kind understanding which the eunuch absorbed as his right. But as the wedding drew nearer and Sporus' hysterics became shriller, they grew a little tired of his antics.

Soft bosoms no longer welcoming his head, Sporus found new ways to attract the light he so craved. Dressed in a long black gown which puddled like ink behind him, one arm swept across his brow, wailing hysterically, Sporus roamed the corridors of the slave complex. He took to grasping onto the arms of passing slaves, beseeching them to dispatch him now for he could not bear to be so betrayed! To see his beloved Nero wed to another! Why he would rather die than let his eyes view such poison! Let the Gods strike him down now with their almighty power!

And thus a new word entered the palace lingo: Sporused.

Sporus was hurt. He was wounded. He was suffering dreadfully. Why would nobody acknowledge it? To this end Sporus' Sporusing widened beyond the unsympathetic slave complex and into the public areas of the palace. It was a particularly noteworthy collision with an ex-consul that led to a firm conclusion: Sporus must be contained. Since then he'd been held in his suite of rooms with two praetorian guards placed outside to prevent any further escapades.

"I don't understand," worried Philo. "You say that he did not come past you?"

"No, definitely not," said Guardsmen Proculus.

Philo gazed about the room, leaning a palm on the wall: solid.

"There's no other way out, though. Not even a window for him to squeeze through."

"Regular mystery it is," offered Guardsman Lucullus. "I think there's magic involved here, sir. I reckon she's a witch and magicked her way out. They can do that, sir, witches. They are pretty cunning."

As an explanation it did not satisfy Philo. He bent down, peering under the couch. An expectedly dark space. Hang on, what was that? He lay on the floor and fished an arm in, his hand closing round the object. Getting to his feet he showed it to the guards.

"It's a shoe."

It was a high heeled sandal with glittering diamonds in the toes and a golden buckle. It could only belong to Sporus.

"Tell me again how you found he was missing."

"Well sir, we got a bit worried about her. We could hear her crying."

"And…banging."

"Banging?"

"Yeah, banging. We thought we'd better check it out, see that the little lady was alright. Not hurting herself or nothing."

"So we came in and she wasn't here."

"Not a sign."

"You both came in?"

"Yes, sir."

Philo looked to the door, then to the couch, then to the guards, asking, "You both came in and you stood about here?"

Philo stepped into the centre of the room, the door behind him, the couch to his right.

"Yeah about that sir. Scratching our heads we were."

Scratching their heads, puzzling it out as Sporus crawled out from under the couch, losing a shoe in the process and nipped out the door behind them, concluded Philo.

***

Felix, Head of Slave Placements and Chief Overseer cracked his knuckles and furrowed his red eyebrows across his prominent nose like two furry caterpillars looking to scrap to the death. In front of him were his slave overseers, the men whose job it was to keep the Imperial workforce working. Order had to be maintained and these were the men that did it. Their tactics were simple: they menaced. Standing directly in front of Felix was the most menacing of them all: Straton.   Of impressive bulk, he was less of a man and more akin to a semi-shaven bear. He might not have possessed claws, but what he did have was a whip. This was hung on his thick leather belt for easy access and had been used to painful effect on generations of palace slaves.

"Right," growled Felix. "The praetorians,"

The overseers jeered at that word, for there was a hefty rivalry between the guard and the overseers, both sides believing themselves to be the premier security force in the palace.

"The praetorians_," began Felix again, injecting a sneer of his own, "were given a eunuch to guard. They were supposed to keep him out of mischief. They failed."

Another round of jeers.

"So now we have the job. The eunuch known as Sporus is on the loose. We need to find him. Now it's a big old palace and we need to be fucking smart about this." Felix tapped a large digit against his temple. "We need to think like Sporus. We need to get into his head and then we'll find him.

"So. I'm a flighty, fancy, poncy, attention seeking, ball-less wonder. I delight in mischief, trouble and mincing about. I've made my escape from my crap, good for nowt praetorian fuckwits and I'm loose in the palace. Which I have no fucking right to be. Where the fuck would I go?"

Felix threw an enquiring look at this gathered team. A series of spectacularly ugly, but blank faces stared back.

Felix scratched at his beard mumbling, "Knew this would be a fucking waste of time, appealing to their fucking intelligence. When was the last time they held an actual thought in their actual heads? HEY HEY! LET'S HAVE SOME FUCKING IDEAS!!!!!"

A hand shot up. "Yes Xagoras."

"Bathroom."

"We don't have bathroom breaks Xagoras. You can piss in a corner. We got fucking WORK TO DO!"

"Sir, I meant the eunuch. If I were a lack ball and I'd given the Guards the slip, I'd probably want to, you know, freshen up a bit."

Felix considered, "Not a bad idea Xagoras, you go check it out."

"Err which bathroom?"

"ALL OF THEM!" bellowed Felix, Xagoras dashing out to search the many, many, many bathrooms that littered all ends of the palace from the Palatine to the Oppian Hill.

"RIGHT! Let's have some suggestions from the rest of you."

"Wardrobe? He lost a shoe, he won't want to be uncoordinated."

"Not bad Pius. You go see to that."

Straton cleared his throat, a sound not unlike an elephant taking a dislike to his trainer in the moment before a fatal tusking.

"MINERVA'S ARSE! You got an idea Straton? That's got to be a fucking first. You get struck by lightning on the way in? Fucking illuminate you, did it? Go on then, where would you go?"

Straton grinned, showing his sharp blackened teeth. "Weddin'. Emperor's weddin'"

Felix's hand shot up and slapped his forehead with a wince inducing thwack for those watching. Oh, Mars' favourite whore! That is exactly where the little fucker would head. Hadn't he been whining and crying all over the palace about being dumped by the Emperor? What better place to fully express his hurt and grief than in front of 500 wedding guests, all the dignitary Rome had to offer and the actual lady that had displaced him as empress?

Felix scrunched his eyes shut as the full horror of a Sporus injected wedding coursed through him. He took a deep breath, filling up his entire barrel of a chest. Then he fixed his eyes on Straton.

"Stop him. Now. By whatever means."

Straton hitched up his belt and grinned.

***

iv.

As Xagoras dashed from bathroom to bathroom, Straton preferred not to exert himself. No point working up a sweat scouring the palace for the eunuch, when he could prop a shoulder against a pillar and wait for Sporus to come to him. The pillar in question was one of twelve that held up the roof of the grand entrance hall to the banqueting suite. The pink marble was ten feet in diameter and thus able to disguise even a man of Straton's impressive bulk from the arriving wedding guests.

One shoulder leant against the marble. Straton's black eyes scanned the crowds of well-dressed dignitaries, their wives and their slaves. The latter on hand to provide assistance, comfort and an arm to hold onto when they all staggered out drunk later in the evening. Straton figured that Sporus would wait until all the guests were settled before making his entrance, for maximum effect. The best way to do that was to sneak in with the guests, hence Straton's vigilance. His eyes moved quickly across the scene, one hand gripping the handle of the whip which hung from his belt.

***

Epaphroditus, having soothed the emperor's concerns over the invented divorce from Poppaea, followed the Imperial entourage to the hall. Calvia's exquisite wedding planning involved Nero and Statilia parading down opposite sides of the entrance hall, following two groups of lyre players; one group plucking a tune for the Emperor and one for the Empress. As the couple approached the door the tunes would meld into one harmonious melody as the happy couple met.

For Epaphroditus this was not a metaphor of Imperial marriage that he recognised. But he admired the organisation of it.

There were no cock ups for Philo to record in his note tablet as the bride and groom met. This was Epaphroditus' first glimpse of Statilia Messalina. Her eyes were blue, her nose small and her lips on the plumpish. She was pretty. Calvia had chosen well. Epaphroditus approved.

Nero too seemed satisfied with Statilia Messalina. Glancing back over his shoulder at Epaphroditus, he mouthed, 'tasty.'

She stood upright as a pillar. Her face neutral, displaying neither fear nor joy, letting Nero take her arm without a flinch. Epaphroditus, though, noted the deep intake of breath that puffed out her breast as the first trumpet sounded.

"Nooooooooooooooooooooooooooo!"

Came a high pitched squeal from the back of the room. From behind a pillar shot Sporus, running full pelt down the centre of the hall. The emperor and empress pivoted.

"What the____?" began Nero.

A thought shared by the trumpet players, who went spectacularly off key.

The guards proved their general uselessness once again by their motionless gawps as Sporus headed towards the Imperial party. Epaphroditus was much quicker off the mark.

"An assassin!" declared the secretary.

He dashed off towards the eunuch before the emperor could recognise him.

Sporus, surprisingly for such a natural coward, was unfazed by the sight of the Emperor's Private Secretary running towards him. He was even unfazed by the two praetorians who finally joined the race. His thoughts were solely concentrated on stopping this pantomime of a wedding.

Nero wouldn't hurt him so, not after he saw how upset his darling Sporus/Poppaea/Whatever was at this betrayal. His eyes were firmly on Epaphroditus, intending to scoot round him at the last moment. Which was why Sporus failed to see Straton slip out from his hiding spot.

Crack. The thong of Straton's whip propelled forward and attached itself round Sporus' ankle. The overseer gave it a hard tug. Thump. Sporus hit the marble floor. The air was oompthed out of him. His chin banged on the ground. A red slash on his ankle bled from Straton's targeted shot.

The overseer grabbed him by the other ankle, dangling him upside down. "Got me eunuch," he grinned.

Epaphroditus, fully engaged on his interception mission, realised with dismay that he was moving too fast to stop in time.

"Minerva's Arse!" he swore, as he careered into Straton, knocking him over.

To fell a man of Straton's size was an astounding feat, but Epaphroditus had no time to dwell on this success since the two praetorians who'd also been in pursuit smacked into the pile of overseer/eunuch/secretarial staff.

The confusion of limbs, whips and swords freed Sporus from Straton's hold, he wriggled out from beneath a yelping praetorian. Giving no thought to the state of his dress, a first for Sporus and one born of his single-minded mission, the eunuch escaped by crawling along the floor, his long nails clicking on the marble as he did.

Epaphroditus, his eye smarting from an accidental encounter with Straton's elbow, struggled to free himself. Seeing Sporus heading towards the emperor's end of the hall, he thrust his foot into a praetorian groin and kicked hard. The guard screamed in presumed agony and it was this pain that no doubt clouded his judgement in such a terrible way. Mistaking Straton for the cause of his throbbing testicles, he yelled, "You ugly basted! I'm going to get you for that!"

In the chronicles of palace history there had scarcely been a more misguided declaration. Or more wrong. As demonstrated when Straton, with the effortless strength that was his hallmark, picked up the guard and threw him at a pillar. There was a sort of crunching sound as praetorian and marble met. A sound Straton seemed intent on repeating, as he picked up the comatose guard again.

Epaphroditus had no time (or indeed inclination) to intervene in Straton's thorough beating, he had a eunuch to catch. By now Sporus was an alarming third of the way across the hall, almost within recognisable distance to the Imperial couple. This was no time for hesitation. Scrambling to his feet he ran and threw himself on top of the eunuch, flattening it.

"Oh no you don't," he hissed in Sporus' ear.

At the far end of the hall the wedding party stood in bemused silence. "What is going on?" asked Statilia.

Nero, keen to appear in charge in front of his soon to be wife, cupped his hands over his mouth and called. "EPAPHRODITUS! WHAT'S GOING ON?" "All under control Caesar," came the call back.

"Well that's good," Nero smiled to Statilia. "Shall we go in?" Taking her arm. There came a perfectly tuned blast from the trumpets and the great doors of the banqueting hall were flung open.

***

v.

Epaphroditus lay prone on the couch. A wet cloth, which he claimed was for his Straton induced black eye, but that was really more connected to his throbbing post wedding induced hangover, was pressed over his face.

It had been quite the wedding and quite the party. With Straton on Sporus minding duty Epaphroditus had been able to relax and enjoy the festivities. He had pulled it off hadn't he? Nero was safely married off. The eunuch would soon be forgotten and back to its normal duties dancing about and irritating the other eunuchs. All was well. Apart from his dry mouth, extremely delicate stomach and the pounding in his cranium.

"There was, sir, a distinct under performance in the catering team," said Philo.

This was hour two of his detailed report into the events of the wedding. Peeking out from under the cloth, Epaphroditus noted a further four note tablets poking out of Philo's satchel.

"The first dishes of roasted pigeon, sir, were not of sufficient crispness. I noted one of the guests, Senator Regulus, make a comment to his wife that he had tasted better when dining with the Consul...."

The secretary gave a pained groan that did not dent Philo's commentary in the slightest.

Interview - with LJ Trafford

Can you tell us a bit about yourself? How long have you been writing and what other jobs have you had?

As a child I had a desperate desire to become an author. Not a writer but an author.

I set about achieving this ambition by half arsedly coming up with stories and never writing them down (until I started on my first book Palatine.)

In the meantime I've had various jobs, including a stint as a tour guide in the Lake District Wordsworth industry. Though this left me with a life long hatred of that poem and those flowers *cough* daffodils *cough* it did train me up in the art of telling a good story. That and the joy of making people laugh for money.

I have been successfully starting books and actually ending them for ten years now. The first completed novel felt like a fluke. But I've written four now, so I might just be getting the hang of it somewhat.

I like to keep my writing life separate from my ordinary life. I have a, sensible, alter ego who does whizzy things with databases and constructs beautiful graphs for a London based organisation. Whilst L.J. writes funny books about Romans and obsesses about the Emperor Domitian all over social media. Occasionally the two meet and it all gets a bit messy.

What is it about Rome that inspires you?

The cor blimey element of it. There are no half measures about Roman emperors: either they're reforming and rebuilding the heck out of Rome and conquering everything in their path. Or they're embarking on ten-hour orgies, indulging in unmentionable behaviour (which all good Roman historians will list in eye popping glory) and thinking they're divine.

Sometimes both. So really I admire their ability to cram a lot of living in. Probably because telly hadn't been invented then.

What inspired you to write this particular story?

In my series of novels I have the recurring character, Sporus who was Nero's most favourite eunuch. So favourite he dressed Sporus up as his dead wife, Poppaea and pretended he/she was the empress.

A delusional emperor who thinks a eunuch is his wife, whilst not having an heir in place, I imagined was quite a challenge for the palace staff. Do you puncture the delusion at the risk of angering the emperor? Or do you go along with it, at the risk of growing dissent against the emperor?

I wanted to explore their solution to the problem, getting Nero quickly remarried!

Can you tell us about your other work inspired by Rome?

I have written four books that cover the tumultuous year of the four emperors, 69AD:

Palatine, Galba's Men, Otho's Regret and Vitellius' Feast.

It is a period rich with battles, massacres, political back stabbing, literal back stabbing and some very bad decisions made all round.

Perfect fiction material.

I write from the viewpoint of the slaves and ex slaves of the palace, because they are on the front line of all this chaos. It is they who have to choose the right side at the right time and fight for survival.

In a nutshell I've rewritten Tacitus' Histories with all the bits he should have put in but didn't. In his elite class of Senators the lives of slaves were not worth recording and sausage/penis gags were socially unacceptable. So I've done him a service really.

I've also written a short story, The Wine Boy set in the Emperor Tiberius' reign. It was my first work to receive a one-star review and thus I am obscenely proud of it.

What do you enjoy most about writing?

The finished product mostly. Writing a book is a hard, hard slog. But I love that shiny paperback in my hand. I also love it when readers contact me to tell me how much they enjoyed my book, that gets me through the dark, dark days of editing.

If you were transported back to the time your story is set, who is the first person you would want to talk to and why?

Nero's favourite eunuch, Sporus. He has all the best gossip in the palace plus a good eye for fashion. I could really do with a make over.

What would you bring back from ancient Rome with you?

I think we've all wondered what Roman food tastes like. So I'm bringing back a dish invented by the Emperor Vitellius. The ingredients are:

"Livers of pike, the brains of pheasants and peacocks, the tongues of flamingoes and the milt of lampreys"

For info, milt of lampreys is eel sperm.

Yum.

If there was one event in the period you could witness (in perfect safety) what would it be?

I would like to see a Nero performance. He gets a lot of sneering from our sources about his singing and poetry. I'd like to see whether they were justified or whether he was a potential winner of Rome's Got Talent.

Why do you think readers are still so thirsty for stories from this period?

I really couldn't say. But I am happy to keep writing them.

What are you writing at the moment?

I am writing a guidebook entitled How to Survive in Ancient Rome.

It was pitched to me as Horrible Histories for Grown ups. So expect top facts and fart gags aplenty.

How important is it for you to be part of a community of writers, and why?

Writing is a very lonesome job and, like sex, you never know if you're doing it right. So it helps to have people who understand the horror of a first draft and can talk you through it.

Also I find historical fiction writers super supportive of each other's work. It's a nice gang to be a member of.

Where can readers find out more about your books?

Amazon is a good place to start. Or my publisher Aeon's website.

Also follow me on Twitter @traffordlj or Facebook. L.J. is very social on social media.

The Praetorian - S.J. Turney

The Renegade

Caere, two days before the Ides of September, 190 AD

'Jove but I'm tired,' the Praetorian said with a sigh, as he slipped out from between the saddle horns and slid down from the back of the ageing white mare. Stretching out sore muscles and stamping life back into his feet, he tied his reins to the rail by the southern edge of the square and turned, torches and oil lamps casting light across his white tunic and reflecting a myriad of shimmering, twinkling stars in the scale armour atop it. He reached out over the saddle bag and the bow slung in a carry-case above it, and patted the coarse white hair of his favourite horse.

'Not long now.' Then, looking across the empty dark square, 'This is all assuming he's still here.'

Caere. A city as old as Rome. Older, some of its prouder citizens would claim. Twenty five miles northwest of the great city as the arrow flies. A provincial shithole right on Rome's doorstep. Rufinus snorted. When had he become so snobbish?

The square was silent and still, the elegant columns of some temple off to one side, public buildings all around, a low parapet at the far, northern edge where a steep escarpment made high city walls unnecessary, and off to the right in the middle distance, a tavern. Warm gold light leeched from the door and half-shuttered windows and the sign – *The Dancing Nymph* – hung above it like a limp scarf in the summer heat.

He stood there for some time, waiting with an ever-increasing sense of impatience. The local town edict called for the tavern to be closing now, though it showed little sign of doing so, from the distant murmur of voices and lyre music emanating from it. The distant patter of footsteps did not distract him.

Expected. Stay on the target.

For just the blink of an eye he turned back to the horse. Atalanta stood alone and content. He nodded and spun back just in time to see the golden rectangle of light blotted out by a burly figure. He couldn't make out the identity. It could be Memmius. He couldn't be sure yet. Tense, he chewed lightly on his lip.

The shape stepped out into the empty square, stopped outside the door and stretched.

Rufinus took a relieved breath. The man was barrel-chested and thick-limbed, short for a soldier, but with a powerful build. Most importantly, he was wearing his uniform, which marked him out every bit as much as Rufinus' own did. His was clean, of course. Memmius' tunic was a stained, shabby thing as befitted a criminal on the run. His armour lacked that giveaway gleam in the tavern's light, suggesting serious rust-pitting and a filthy patina. Of course, if wasn't his physical cleanliness that set Rufinus' teeth on edge, but the corrosion in the man's heart.

The shabby Praetorian in the doorway's light turned, taking in the square, and stopped sharp at the sight of a white-clad figure beside a horse at the square's southern end.

'Memmius,' Rufinus called out in a clear, authoritative tone.

The figure remained still, only his hand moving to the belt at his waist.

'The road has ended now, Memmius. You've had a good run, but you must have known I'd catch up with you.'

'Fuck off, Rufinus.'

Good. Every bit of rancour the man exhibited made hunting him that little bit easier.

'Memmius, we know who you are and what you've done. There's no going back. The Guard has already struck your name from its lists, and the frumentarii have your name on their tongues. If you give me the papers, I could be persuaded to allowing you a noble end, without the knives in the palace cellars.'

'I have done nothing wrong, Rufinus.'

The younger man laughed coldly. 'Now we both know that's not true, Memmius. You were on Cleander's leash for over a year and, since his fall, trails have led to every corrupt little man in his web. Illegal confiscation of property, falsification of

160

documents, the murder of seven innocent civilians during the Circus riot and, though proof has yet to turn up, we all know you were behind the death of a praetorian optio when you fled the fortress. You're going to die, Memmius. The sentence has already been passed in Rome, but you could save yourself torture and the display of your mangled corpse if you hand me those papers in your pack and then throw yourself on your sword. A last, redemptive display of *Romanitas*?'

He couldn't make out Memmius' expression, but he could almost hear the sneering pull of the man's lip. He sighed.

'Don't make this difficult.'

The big man turned back to the door. 'Lentulus? Time to earn your money.'

Rufinus' eyes narrowed as he watched the light blotted out again, this time by a man with the same body shape but a good two feet taller. Damn, but this Lentulus was big.

'Lentulus is Raetian,' Memmius shouted. 'He began his career by tearing the arms off deserters for the governor's pleasure. All I want is to be left alone, Rufinus. To disappear. If you run, we can both still walk away from this.'

Rufinus shook his head. 'That's *Centurion* Rufinus, you shit.'

In reply, Memmius jabbed a finger in Rufinus' direction and the huge lunk turned and began to amble, gorilla-like, across the square. In his huge ham fist was a hammer of the sort a blacksmith used to bash out large plates of iron. A monster just like its owner.

'I warn you not to interfere, Lentulus,' Rufinus called out. 'Memmius is a criminal. Whatever he paid you won't be worth the result.'

But words were clearly not going to stop the Raetian. In a moment of uncertainty, Rufinus wasn't entirely sure what *would* stop him. Memmius showed no sign of flight. He was confident in the ability of his hired muscle, clearly. Rufinus frowned, sizing up the big man as he ambled closer. Very strong. *Very* strong. Rufinus could see the muscle tone. There was no fat on the man. Enormous. Bald and beardless, perhaps to leave nothing to grasp in a fight. His only weapons were the hammer and his fist, the former secured by a loop of leather around his wrist to prevent its loss. He did not seem to be favouring either leg, stood straight, and both arms swung as he walked. No obvious flaws.

On a whim, Rufinus took three quick steps left and then six right before returning to the middle. The big man's gaze followed him perfectly. No imperfection in his sight, then. This was going to be a tough one.

He drew his blade with a throaty rasp and drew a few figure eights in the air, readying himself.

Lentulus closed.

Memmius watched like a spectator at the arena.

'Don't do this,' Rufinus said in quieter, more serious tones as the giant closed on him.

Lentulus said nothing; came on. His tunic was grey and knee length, and he wore dun coloured breeches beneath, old military boots completing the ensemble. Rufinus was glad he'd not come up against this bastard in a match when they'd both been in the legions.

Still, back in those days they had fought by certain rules. Now, rules were for other people.

Slowly, he slid the sword back into its sheath. Defending himself was one thing, but Lentulus may have done nothing wrong, other than accept coin from the wrong praetorian. And the death of a bystander created far too much paperwork. Besides, watching the big man's lumbering, slightly bow-legged walk had sealed his plan anyway.

Lentulus picked up speed now, most of the way across the square, bursting into a run. A legionary of old, marching into battle and then into double time before the charge. Just like Rufinus, conditioned to the tactics of the legion. Unlike Rufinus, he'd probably not spent the last decade dealing with renegade generals, imperial conspirators, Sarmatian cannibals and murderous cavalrymen.

As the huge man closed on Rufinus, his left arm came in reflexively, bent at the elbow as if shielding himself, the great mallet sweeping out and ready to swing. Rufinus readied, braced with all his weight on the balls of his feet and knees very slightly bent. His right fist flexed and then balled into a powerful fist. Almost a decade, but everything was still natural.

The big man attacked. His great mallet gripped tight came round in a powerful swing. In anticipation, the Raetian had lunged slightly forward, granting him that little bit extra swing, for it would be natural for his victim to duck back from that swinging death.

Rufinus had not leaned back, though.

Knees already bent, he instead dropped to a crouch and swung that powerful fist upwards as the big man towered over him, arm over-extended, eyes wide with shock.

Rufinus' knuckles ploughed with force into the Raetian's groin, for he was now at the perfect height, and Lentulus' forward momentum only added to the power of the blow. Something made an unpleasant cracking noise and Rufinus tried not to ponder on what he'd just done. Some things didn't deserve thinking about.

He remained crouched as the Raetian simply fell over him, an unearthly howl issuing from his throat as he collapsed to the floor face first, hammer left to swing on the strap as his hands reached down to his ruined genitals.

Rufinus waited until he heard the man crash fully to the stones, the howl descending to an agonised whimper, and then slowly unfolded and rose to his feet, dusting off his white tunic sleeves. Memmius remained in place. Rufinus still couldn't see his face, but he could picture the expression well enough.

'I wasn't always a praetorian, Memmius. Twenty two bouts in the ring representing the First Cohort of the Tenth Gemina. Of course, the testicles were out of bounds then.'

Still, Memmius didn't move. Shock?

'I know you have contacts, Memmius. I know there are others still to be found. Who knows, if you're of sufficient help, perhaps the authorities might commute your sentence.'

That was a lie, of course. Every spider in Cleander's web was a dead man walking since the corrupt chamberlain's fall. But anything that might make this easier.

Memmius moved suddenly. Rufinus sighed as the man turned and ran.

'Oh, come on.'

The squat criminal was making for the north of the square, and Rufinus broke into a jog and then a run, chasing him down, leaving the big Raetian on the floor nursing his broken manhood. He slowed, eyes widening, as he watched Memmius accelerate as he approached that low parapet to the square's north. Surely not?

He stared in disbelief as Memmius reached the wall and vaulted over it without a moment's hesitation. With an irritated exhale, Rufinus jogged across the rest of the square.

To the north he could see the dark shapes of the southern Etrurian hills like rolling waves beneath the inky sky. His eyes dropped from the horizon as he neared the parapet. They took in the wide, wooded valley below the town, with its vast, ancient cemetery, a narrow river that was little more than a stream at this time of year looping around below Caere. Then the slope, gradually rising in steepness as it neared the wall upon which he stood, and finally to the twenty foot drop from the edge that made a city wall here largely unnecessary.

He took in the figure of Memmius, half-running, half-bouncing and rolling down that slope. He would be taking a battering, but a man with his build would endure it. As long as he had broken nothing critical in that first twenty feet the rest would just be pain and discomfort and Rufinus knew, better than most, how pain could be endured. He shook his head in disbelief. Did Memmius truly think he could still run? Had Rufinus not already proved that was not the case?

Something caught his eye, and his gaze jerked up from that tumbling white figure.

A light had burst into life somewhere in the cemetery, a twinkle of golden light in the dark. A sneaking suspicion fell upon Rufinus, a suspicion seemingly confirmed when another twinkling light began in a different part of the great ancient necropolis. Then another. And another.

Four fires.

He'd always known that Memmius would have accomplices. Indeed, he'd been certain that the papers the renegade had taken from the praetorian fortress when he ran would incriminate several others. But oddly it had not occurred to him that perhaps they had already fled and were with him.

Five men at least, and that was just assuming one man per fire. All dangerous, trained praetorians, no doubt. Of course, Rufinus had taken steps. He was no idiot, but still it seemed the odds had just swung a little in Memmius' favour. Indeed, the fugitive praetorian was now on his feet properly, running down the lower slopes to splash into the stream on his way to the graveyard, shouting to his companions.

Rufinus peered down at the archaic cemetery, home of the bodies of Etruscan noblemen before the coming of Rome, with its drum-shaped houses of the dead separated by deep shadowy streets, and he sighed.

His hand reached down by his side and something large, black and very hairy appeared beneath his fingers. Rufinus scratched the dog's head gently.

'I may need your help tonight after all, old friend.'

The Hunt

Rufinus cleared his throat quietly as he tied Atalanta up once more, looping her reins around a thick branch of an ancient old yew tree standing guard at the entrance of the cemetery. His fingers reached up to the large, heavy leather bag holding the bulky cheiroballista, danced around the fastenings for a moment, and then reached up to the other bag, unfastening it and hauling it over and onto his shoulder. It clonked, chinked and rattled with deadly contents. He'd never have carried such things before he'd signed on with the frumentarii.

The eyes, ears and daggers of the emperor, the frumentarii were committed to seeking out treachery and crime among the imperial army, often hiding among their number. Rufinus had been a praetorian for six years before his faked death, and only with Cleander's fall had he returned to the ranks of the imperial guard, this time with a remit from that shadowy imperial force to cut out corruption.

He hefted the bag.

'How things change eh?'

165

He looked around as shadows danced and moved among the trees in the poor moonlight. Atalanta nickered quietly and Acheron, the great black Sarmatian hound that went everywhere with his praetorian master, mooched around the grass, waiting.

'Very well,' he said to those shadows, 'let's hunt.'

There was something extremely eerie about the cemetery, as Rufinus and his companion turned and paced towards the street of the dead. What secrets and ghosts did those ancient tombs hold, some of them a thousand years old, hailing from a day when Rome was little more than a village on a hill? It was truly a necropolis – a *city* of the dead, whole lines of Etruscan nobility housed in those golden stone cylinders topped with a dome of earth.

Not just the nobles, either. The ordinary folk had their tombs here, chiselled caves in the rock with remarkably ornate doors leading out onto the streets in ordered rows. As Rufinus moved into the edge of the cemetery, he shivered. He could half imagine those doors opening and their mouldering occupants stepping out for a walk through the streets in a parody of life.

He shook off the notion and rolled his shoulders. This was no time to get distracted with fantastic imaginings.

The hunt was on.

Titus Annaeus stalked along the street. He was not a man usually given to wild worries, but this place put the shits up him. When they'd abandoned Rome, he'd advocated a fast ship to Hispania, but the others had been oddly determined to stay local. Shadows seemed to move like real people here, and he shivered for the hundredth time.

As if to reassure himself, he turned and looked back. Far away he could see the glow of the fire they had left, the comforting shadows of Caelius and Fabius blocking out the glow. Good. Three of them would take down the praetorian, so long as the ghosts didn't get them first.

A strange noise ahead drew his attention and he squinted into the darkness. Nothing. He turned, wondering whether the other two had heard it, and his heart skipped a beat. Where a moment ago there had been two shapes silhouetted in the firelight, now there was only one.

'Fuck. Where's Fabius?'

Caelius looked around in surprise. 'He was here a moment ago. He'll have gone down the next road, cutting them off.'

Annaeus nodded, though he was less certain. In his head he saw crumbling Etruscan revenants eating his friend. He shivered again and looked carefully at all the shadows. His attention was so riveted upon the dancing shapes ahead and the sounds of rustling tree branches and leaves that he failed to spot the danger until it was too late. The two inch spike of the caltrop sank into the sole of his foot, passing with ease through the leather boot and deep into his flesh. He yelped in pain and came to a stop. Lifting his foot to examine the barbed iron nightmare sticking out of it, his gaze fell upon the barely-visible shapes of others, scattered in the dark of the alleyway.

'Shit.'

He tried to pull the spike out, but the barb was caught on something and it was agony. Panicked, now, he hopped over to the wall of the street and leaned against ancient stone, turning to warn Caelius.

He was just in time to see his friend die. A great, black shape, growling with all the hate of Tarterus, leapt from a doorway and hit the other man so hard he was thrown across the alley with a cry to slam against the far side and fold up on the floor, screaming as a hound the size of a small bear began to tear at him with impunity.

'Fuck, fuck, fuck,' Annaeus said with feeling. Wincing, he yanked at the caltrop. It came free sharply, carrying pieces of both boot and foot with it. Blood started to flow. Annaeus didn't care. He should have given himself up back in Rome. All he'd ever done was push a rioter down some steps and kick him a few times. He'd probably have been able to talk his way out of a sentence, especially if he'd sold out the others. Why had he ever listened to Memmius?

Carefully, trying with great difficulty to keep his eyes on both the underfoot dangers ahead and the black monster eating

Caelius behind, he tested his foot. He could walk, but it would hurt like Tarterus itself, and he was losing a lot of blood.

Carefully, he took several steps. At least among the caltrops, the beast would probably not follow. He breathed a sigh of relief as he reached the corner and slipped around it, out of sight of the black monster.

A gladius slid into his armpit with ease as his hand rested on the ancient stones beside him. He looked up in shock, his own blade falling from his hands.

No. If the praetorian had been at the back and picked off Fabius, how in Hades had he got round in front so fast? It was a question destined to remain unanswered, as the blade neatly skewered Annaeus' heart and stilled it. He died with little more than a sigh of regret, crumpling to the ground.

Rufinus climbed the steps of the nearest, most decorative cylinder tomb, reaching the turf dome atop it just as the sounds of the approaching men became clear, suggesting they had emerged from the side street. Hefting the heavy items, he scrambled across the turf to the far side of the roof. He'd no idea how to employ them beyond the obvious, for he'd never had such a weapon in combat; never even seen one used, in fact. In a way, he wished he could simply use his sword for all this, but even with the advantages he could claim, the odds were just too stacked against him. He had to be as sneaky as they – more so – if he wanted victory tonight.

As he reached the edge of the roof he saw the two men, both in praetorian white and both wearing drab cloaks over the top. It was far from a cold night, so both men wore what they did to help conceal them in the shadows. It didn't work, especially from a high vantage point like this.

'Just run back to Rome,' one of the men shouted, hands cupped around his mouth. 'You'll never get out of here alive if you dawdle.'

Rufinus chewed his lips. Two men. Ten plumbatae. If he aimed, then he would only get one off at a time and the men might just get away. If he didn't, what were his chances of success? But then the man who had given him them, his mentor and friend in the frumentarii, had told him to throw them up like a wheat shower at a wedding. Rufinus smiled to think of the analogy, given than 'frumentarius' meant 'grain man'.

Had to be quick.

Taking a shallow breath, he gripped five of the heavy iron darts in each hand and gave a strong underarm throw. They hurtled up into the night air, all but silent, and plummeted back down the moment they reached their apex. Muttering to one another, the two men never heard the weapons cast upwards, and became aware of the peril only as they fell. Each dart consisted of a sharp iron spike on the end of a heavy lead ball, a tail with three fins on it stretching off behind.

Rufinus watched, impressed.

The darts fell in a cloud of ten hissing iron barbs. Two slammed into the man who had shouted his threat, and one into the second. The other seven thudded to the packed earth of the street. Three seemed to be adequate. Neither man was wearing a helmet, for the simple expediency of better vision in the dark streets. But they'd not been looking up.

One dart thudded straight into the top of a man's head with an audible crack. He concertinaed to the ground in a heartbeat, unconscious, his skull cracked and blood bubbling up. The other man avoided the more direct wound, though might perhaps have preferred it. One dart tore the flesh from his forehead, cheek and chin before falling away and the other thudded down into the crook of his collar bone and shoulder, the spike digging half a hand-length into his flesh. He screamed and clutched at the dart lodged in his shoulder, bits of face flapping from the falling dart's damage and blood welling up from the torso.

Rufinus almost felt sorry for the man. Almost. He was not a man given to cruelty, though he was as comfortable as the next man with a gladius in hand. But these men were each and every one criminals. The creatures of Cleander, who had murdered innocent civilians in the name of their chamberlain master. Men who had robbed and killed and cheated with the blessing of the most powerful man in Rome, and who now died in his name.

The screaming man turned as Rufinus landed behind him, knees bent for impact, and rose once more only to deliver a killing blow with his sword. If anything, the disfigured man looked relieved as the blade sank in.

Leaving the two men to die swiftly, he moved off, Acheron padding out of a side alley to fall in alongside him, panting and with matted, glistening hair. The two turned a corner and found two more mangled bodies. Rufinus didn't even remember these two.

Rubelius had changed his mind about all this. The screaming of his friends had been bad enough, but when he'd found Ahala's body lying in a doorway with the garrotte still deep in his neck, almost to the point of severing it, he'd had enough. He knew they'd never stop looking for him. He'd killed a senator's wife and child in the press the day Cleander fell, not to mention the many, many lesser crimes. But he could run. He'd run forever if he needed to. But he wouldn't fall to this praetorian and his beast. They had to be working for the grain men, he decided.

He had a cousin with a boat up the coast at Centum Cellae. Less than twenty miles. He could be there in time to leave at first light. And he'd certainly had enough of this damned city of the dead that seemed to claim new inhabitants with every heartbeat.

He could see how close he was to the edge of the cemetery now, and given the screaming way back behind him, the mad bastard hunting them had to be far off. He turned the last corner to the cemetery's end with profound relief.

There was an ominous click.

The bolt came so fast that Rubelius hadn't even time to panic. Six inches of sharp iron backed with an ash shaft and twin flights slammed so hard into his chest that his armour ruptured, shining scales raining down to the ground like an exploded fish. The bolt drove into his innards and would have passed straight through had it not lost sufficient momentum to become lodged in the armour at his back. He stared, eyes wide, at the rare, hand-held cheiroballista, its drawstring not snapped tight, all tension lost as it sent its whistling death at the hapless fugitive.

It would have been nice to have got on the boat, Rubelius thought wistfully, as blood pumped from his chest and spilled between his lips.

Memmius stood at the heart of the cemetery. There was no running away, he knew. How the mad bastard was killing off his men he couldn't say, but the screams all over the place made it clear that was what was happening. Still, they were expendable. Everyone was. If life serving Cleander had taught him anything, it had taught him that.

He glanced left and right. Catulus stood in the shadows to his left, and on the far side Piso. Both were well hidden. Memmius stood in the bright firelight, daring Rufinus. He knew the younger praetorian, remembered him from the old days, before his return from the dead. He also knew that the young man clung to a sense of honour that would see confrontation and end in his death.

Sure enough, against a tapestry of distant screams a shush of metal scales announced Rufinus' arrival. He stepped from a dark street. Memmius frowned for a moment at the strange *whup, whup* noise he could hear, but then saw the sling languidly circling in the younger officer's hand.

He smiled and gave the very slightest of nods.

An arrow thrummed from somewhere to his left. It struck Rufinus in the arm. His scale shirt and the leather pteruges stopped serious wounding, but the sling went loose, the stone slamming away into the darkness and the leather weapon falling from numb fingers.

'Oh dear. Are we running out of tricks now, Rufinus?'

The young centurion grunted in pain.

'You're strong, Rufinus. And sharp too. But there are three of us.'

At the cue, his companions stepped from the shadows. Catulus had another arrow nocked, and Piso held a sword in each hand. They were his best. Saved for the last.

'Two,' Rufinus said, and coughed at the pain.

'What?'

'Two, not three.'

Memmius' head shot left sharply, just in time to see something huge and black slam into Catulus, the bow falling away, arrow hurtling off across the ground harmlessly. Catulus gave a throaty scream that ended in an ominous snapping noise from the shadows.

He was shaken. He would never admit it, but he'd felt confident, and now he felt it melting away. Still, he knew where the dog was now, and Rufinus would be working with only one arm.

'Two,' he agreed. 'Still enough.'

'Assumption is a dangerous thing, Memmius.'

'What?' Uncertainty arose again.

'I assumed you'd be alone, I have to admit. But the problem is that you assumed the same thing.'

There was a strange wooden clonk, and Memmius looked right in time to see Piso's face disappear in a cloud of pink and red, the iron and wood bolt carrying brain matter as it emerged from the back of his head to clonk against the golden stone wall.

Piso fell, dead before he hit the floor, and a new figure stepped from the shadows, a hand-held cheiroballista in his hand, which he was reloading already. The figure was clad only in a black tunic with leather subarmalis, his white hair shining in the firelight, the dancing flames picking out his disconcerting mismatched eyes, one green, the other black as Tarterus.

Panic began to build now. This wasn't how it was supposed to go.

'Come on,' smiled Rufinus. 'You didn't think I could have done all this alone? And this man is far more inventive than I.' He nodded across at the black figure, who wore one ornament: a silver brooch in the shape of a wheat sheaf.

Frumentarius. The grain men.

Memmius shuddered. 'I can tell you much. My life could buy you many others.'

'I doubt there is much,' Rufinus countered. 'You've brought all your cronies here. If there was another conspirator you truly trusted, you'd have brought them too. I think you're almost worthless now, Memmius. Your value diminished with every scream.'

'He might still know something,' the black-clad man noted.

Rufinus shook his head. 'Not enough. This man butchered an entire family on the road from Rome the day Cleander fell. It's taken me months to identify him and track him down. It ends tonight.'

Memmius nodded. 'Well if I'm to die, it'll be your black friend here to take me in, Rufinus. With that arm you'll not beat me.'

'Quite right,' Rufinus smiled darkly as he started to pace forwards.

With a thud, the frumentarius loosed his cheiroballista again. Oddly, Memmius had almost written off the man, focusing on Rufinus, but the iron-tipped bolt tore a large chunk from his right bicep and he yelped as his sword scattered away.

'Now we're even,' Rufinus snarled, and broke into a run.

Memmius readied himself as best he could. He was a strong man, heavily built. But he knew he was in trouble. Rufinus was a boxer by training. The younger man was on him in a trice and Memmius managed to land just one solid blow before the repeated pounding of Rufinus' left fist started to drive the sense from him. He gasped as he fell backwards to the ground, but his hunter came with him, falling on top, fist still pounding. Memmius felt his eye close up, swollen and ruined, his lip split, cheek bone broken. He briefly saw the younger man's fist as it pulled back for another blow, and it was torn in several places from punches, but most of the blood coating had to be Memmius'.

He gurgled a desperate plea.

The rain of blows continued unabated for ten more heartbeats, until Memmius felt certain there was no more agony to feel. Then suddenly it stopped. With his remaining eye and through pain-flooded senses, he watched Rufinus being hauled off him. The black-clad man was there. A saviour? Among the frumentarii?

He felt silent gratitude, for he could not speak through his smashed teeth, ruined lips and broken jaw. But his ears still worked, and one eye, and he tried in vain to shake his head as the grain man said to Rufinus: 'Enough. It ends now.

The cold steel of the frumentarius' sword plunged down into Memmius' chest, and he lay transfixed, broken and dying.

'Next time you get to carry the heavy ballista,' the man said to Rufinus. 'Now where's your damn dog?'

Memmius expired and, in the end, if felt like something of a relief.

Interview with SJ Turney

Can you tell us a bit about yourself? How long have you been writing and what other jobs have you had?

Ha. I've had the weirdest, most eclectic career path, from carrying paint cans and gravel sacks, through counting sheep and selling cars, to designing logistics databases and managing networks. Rome and history have always been central to my life, though. Writing seriously came late, with my first attempt at a novel in 2003. I've never looked back.

What is it about Rome that inspires you?

Of all the cultures, in western history at least, Rome is the most immersive and the best recorded, and has substantial remains still to be found. In it, we can find both echoes of our current world and also the roots from which it has grown. Moreover, while many might cite Greece or Egypt as similar, Rome was such an inclusive world that it swiftly encompassed those cultures, adding them to its own.

What inspired you to write this particular story?

I love writing Rufinus. He has become a close friend since the series started. Writing something in the world of Praetorian is like putting on a pair of comfortable old slippers. At the end of the last book, Rufinus takes on the mammoth task of rooting out corruption in the Guard, and in the next book he will face the conclusion of that task, dealing with the end of Commodus's reign and the utter fall of the Praetorians thereafter. I wanted to begin examining what he was facing, and the more I imagined this story, the more it began to look like First Blood, but that's great. First Blood was a great movie.

Can you tell us about your other work inspired by Rome?

Most of my work is military in nature, with the Marius' Mules series following the campaigns of Julius Caesar from 58 to 44 BC, the Praetorian series (of which this tale is now a part) telling the story of a young Praetorian during the reign of Commodus, and my children's series beginning with Crocodile Legion, telling of two kids with a century of legionaries in Hadrianic Egypt. I have also written two novels about the Roman emperors who suffered Damnatio Memoriae (Caligula and Commodus), reconstructing the man without the monster.

What do you enjoy most about writing?

Since childhood I have always been a storyteller. I used to run Dungeons and Dragons games, building worlds and plots and characters. I continually brim with tales waiting to be told, and there is little more satisfying than putting those tales on paper and hearing that someone else has enjoyed them.

If you were transported back to the time your story is set, who is the first person you would want to talk to and why?

Simple. I would want to talk to the emperor himself. To Commodus. Having spent the last couple of years studying him and trying to reconstruct the real man despite the anti-Commodian propaganda following his death, I would love to hear it from the horse's mouth, so to speak. I want to know how close to the truth I've managed.

What would you bring back from ancient Rome with you?

I don't know whether this counts, but what I'd really like is to find someone (probably an engineer) who knows what the damned enigmatic 'dodecahedrons' that are found across the empire actually were. I would bring back the answer to that riddle. To me they appear to be measures for pipes or something similar, but there are so many theories. I want to know what they actually are!

If there was one event in the period you could witness (in perfect safety) what would it be?

I think after having written so many battles of the period, and having been a legionary reenactor testing out theories, I would love to watch the battles of Bedriacum, with legionaries fighting one another in the year of the four emperors. I would be able to finally say with confidence 'ah yes, we got it right', or 'damn it, but we got that wrong.' And in that battle you have the cross section of the entire Roman military, infantry and cavalry, legion, auxilia and even Praetorians.

Why do you think readers are still so thirsty for stories from this period?

Rome seems to be timeless. Historical and literary trends come and go, but Rome has remained a fascination since the age of enlightenment and the first forays into archaeology and translating ancient works. It never dates. And moreover, there remains the unprecedented ability to draw parallels between Rome and the modern world, which makes it familiar as well as exciting.

What are you writing at the moment?

Having just finished the latest Marius' Mules volume, dealing with Caesar's Alexandrian War, I am gearing up for both volume 5 of Praetorian, as I described above, and a non-fiction work on the great general Gnaeus Julius Agricola.

How important is it for you to be part of a community of writers, and why?

In my early days of releasing my tales into the world, I imagined the writing community to be highly competitive and self-absorbed. You grow up with tales of reclusive authors and of plagiarism and the like. What I have found as that world unfolded is quite the opposite. The support and comradeship between authors – especially those of historical fiction – is impressive, total and most welcome. Cross-promotion and help I have both received and given out in swathes. It truly is a community, and I wouldn't want to be without it. I have made lifelong friends in this business.

Where can readers find out more about your books?

www.simonturney.com is my website, sjat.wordpress.com my blog, www.facebook.com/SJATurney my facebook page and @SJATurney my twitter account.

*

Made in the USA
Middletown, DE
10 September 2020